"I..." She was abou[t]
too late.

He was too close and her words dried up on her lips, then he was kissing her far too deeply and desperately for her to even think, let alone speak.

So *this* was what Marianne felt, she heard her own inner girl gasp as if she was sixteen again. No wonder her sister had left everything she knew behind to find her Daniel and stay true to what they had together. It was impossible to turn your back on something as wonderful if there was a chance of a future behind it.

Grown up and very adult as she was now, Viola felt her breath stall and her head spin. The vital life force in him spoke to the one in her and the very air felt as if they had to share it now his mouth was on hers, as if they could not breathe fully without one another. Her knees wobbled and her head went somewhere new, but he was her strength and security under all the strangeness of this feeling. He raised his head to gaze down at her as if he was trying to hang on to some reason she was delighted to see the back of.

"I can't pretend not to want you any longer," he told her as if this had been a long time coming for him as well.

Author Note

Welcome to the third book in my Yelverton trilogy, about the son and two daughters of a country parson. An author should love all her characters equally but Viola Yelverton's hero, Sir Harry Marbeck, is one of my favorites. He is young and dashing and damaged, and it's no wonder Viola yearns for far more from her handsome employer than a cool and proper governess ought to even dream about.

I hope you enjoy reading about the reluctant but, in the end, irresistible attraction between Viola and Harry as his three lively young wards drag them through enough mischief and drama to force them to take a long hard look at what really matters in life and seize the day.

ELIZABETH BEACON

—

The Governess's Secret Longing

HARLEQUIN
HISTORICAL

HARLEQUIN®
HISTORICAL™

Recycling programs
for this product may
not exist in your area.

ISBN-13: 978-1-335-50591-0

The Governess's Secret Longing

Copyright © 2020 by Elizabeth Beacon

For questions and comments about the quality of this book,
please contact us at CustomerService@Harlequin.com.

Harlequin Enterprises ULC
22 Adelaide St. West, 40th Floor
Toronto, Ontario M5H 4E3, Canada
www.Harlequin.com

Printed in U.S.A.

Elizabeth Beacon has a passion for history and storytelling and, with the English West Country on her doorstep, never lacks a glorious setting for her books. Elizabeth tried horticulture, higher education as a mature student, briefly taught English and worked in an office before finally turning her daydreams about dashing piratical heroes and their stubborn and independent heroines into her dream job: writing Regency romances for Harlequin Historical.

Books by Elizabeth Beacon

Harlequin Historical

The Black Sheep's Return
A Wedding for the Scandalous Heiress
A Rake to the Rescue
The Duchess's Secret

The Yelverton Marriages

Marrying for Love or Money?
Unsuitable Bride for a Viscount
The Governess's Secret Longing

A Year of Scandal

The Viscount's Frozen Heart
The Marquis's Awakening
Lord Laughraine's Summer Promise
Redemption of the Rake
The Winterley Scandal
The Governess Heiress

Visit the Author Profile page
at Harlequin.com for more titles.

Chapter One

March 1813

'How is Emma?' Sir Harry Marbeck asked Miss
Thibett's famous junior teacher and told himself
he was glad they were talking privately in a sunny
spring garden far too cold for impropriety.

Although, from the look of her stern cap and
sludge-coloured gown, Miss Yelverton did not encourage impropriety in any weather. Best not to think
about breaking the rules with her wary gaze on him.
She already looked as if she had been asked to meet
a hungry tiger in the headmistress's garden instead
of a grieving baronet. Best not to think about pounc-
ing on her to confirm her darkest suspicions about
him either, or wonder how it would feel to unwrap
her stern draperies layer by intriguing layer to find
the real woman underneath. Except it might be too
late not to think any of that after seeing the dreams

and promise in her sky-blue eyes when she first met his gaze, as if she was holding her breath as well.

She had come bustling out of Miss Thibett's private quarters, eager to be done with this interruption to her busy day, then halted in her tracks and eyed him as if she was astonished not to have been warned he was dangerous. It only took an instant for her defences to go back up, but he still saw an eager and yearning young woman behind her stiff façade. Now he could not get that version of her out of his mind. Did she truly believe a dire gown and stiff manner could blind a red-blooded male to the real woman under the disguise?

Well, she might be deluded about her neat figure and astonishing blue eyes becoming invisible because of it, but he had to look at her as just one more task on the list he must work his way through if his three wards were to feel safe and cared for again. Perhaps he ought to look elsewhere for a governess. He could always apologise for troubling her and go away again.

'Emma is well in herself, but distraught at the loss of her parents,' she said carefully, as if she had to consider every word before she said it. 'Your letter saying you would come for her as soon as you could did much to reassure her she had not been forgotten.'

Something told him she truly cared about Emma, so perhaps he was wrong and Emma's scheme could work, if he kept as chilly a distance from this woman as she was sure to do from him. Maybe if he pretended hard enough that he had never seen the real Miss Yelverton, he could forget the vibrant young woman behind the aloof schoolmistress. He had Emma's tear-stained letter in his pocket to say how dearly his eldest ward wanted this guarded female to stay part of her life, and Emma needed every ounce of security he could find for her right now. He would do anything he could to make her happy. If putting aside his doubts and trying to win over this young woman was what it took to make her feel better, then so be it.

Somehow it had become his job to win Miss Yelverton over. Now all he had to do was convince her that her future lay at Chantry Old Hall with him and his unexpected family of three wards and a tricky maiden aunt. He felt a rueful smile threaten at the thought of the latter, despite Miss Yelverton's sceptical gaze on him and his genuine grief for his cousin Christian and Chris's wife, Jane. Miss Tamara Marbeck, his late and unlamented father's little sister, had turned up on his doorstep with a vast mountain of baggage the day after news of Chris's death reached her. She glared at Harry as if all this chaos must be his fault, then told him she might have failed him as a boy, but she was damned if she would leave the next generation of Marbeck waifs to men who were always supposed to know better and somehow never did.

'I assume the funeral has taken place,' Miss Yelverton said, as if she had been searching for the right words while the silence stretched between them and he struggled with his grief and inner demons.

Any desire to smile faded and he could only nod,

because there were no right words. The sight of two coffins in the church, where his cousin Christian married his Jane so joyfully, was burnt into his memory, but he could not talk about it. Chris was buried alongside his wife for eternity and Harry Marbeck had the happiness and welfare of three orphans on his conscience. Nobody was less suited to the task, but somehow he must muddle through until Chris's children were old enough to run their own lives.

'I am very glad you did not send for Emma as soon as it happened. It has never seemed quite right to me that young children are expected to be trotted out at the wake after losing one parent, let alone two,' Miss Yelverton added uneasily, alerting him to the fact that it was high time he took on his half of this conversation.

'I refused to subject them to that or the gossip that went with it,' he said with a grimace for people who picked over the misery of others for their entertainment.

'Quite right, but why did you ask to see me alone, Sir Harry?'

He had to plead with her headmistress and mentor and explain his errand before the lady admitted it could be the perfect answer to Emma's need for her home at this tragic time if Miss Yelverton returned to the Cotswolds with them, even if it would leave Miss Thibett short of a valued teacher in the middle of the school year.

'I admit I am surprised Miss Thibett sanctioned this meeting. We have never met before and have

nothing in common but your eldest ward,' Miss Yelverton added with none of the polite shilly-shallying
he had expected as she met his bland look.

'Are you aware my late cousin and his wife sent
Emma here to stop her being a responsible big sister all the time at home?' he asked, floundering his
way around a task when he most needed to be direct
and decisive.

Confound it, he had not had any problem finding the right things to say to pretty women since he
was a scrubby schoolboy, but this one threatened to
render him a stuttering and silent buffoon and he
did not even know why. Of course, she was very far
from the picture he had conjured in his head on his
way here, but he had met plenty of lovely women
without feeling blown off course by them. Yet this
young woman pretending to be older, plainer and
more fearsome had him in such a stew of masculine
need and contradiction.

No, he had just won that argument with himself.
She was not a young woman—she was a potential
governess. She mattered to Emma and that was all he
needed to know. He reached for Sir Harry Marbeck's
famous detachment and dash, but the easy words he
tried out in his head still felt wrong for this sensually
innocent, warily defended female. He stood silent
and risked her giving up and going away before he
found the right words to persuade her she must help
him rebuild the children's broken lives.

And to think he had been waiting out here to ruthlessly charm some fussy middle-aged lady into doing

whatever he wanted. The girl had certainly knocked the smugness out of him—and serve him right—but being tongue-tied was not a novelty he was enjoying. He frowned at a clump of daffodils innocently blooming in a corner. Emma's letter in his pocket reminded him he needed Miss Yelverton at Chantry Old Hall, and she was hardly likely to agree if he admitted he was so thrown by the difference between her and the dried-up little sparrow of a woman he had expected that he felt like an overgrown schoolboy at his first grown-up party.

'Yes, Miss Thibett said so when Emma joined my class. I was puzzled as to why such an obviously well-loved child had been sent away from her home,' she replied with a cautious look, as if to say *What of it, Sir Harry Marbeck?*

The sun came back out from behind the swift clouds and lit up a silvery gold curl that had escaped whatever captivity she consigned the rest to when she dressed this morning. He wanted to reach out and touch it to see if it felt as soft, yet full of vitality, as it looked. Had the woman no idea ducking her head and presenting him with the top of a snowy but unadorned cap only intrigued him more? Hiding the rest of her face only highlighted the neat fullness of her mouth and made it even more tempting to dip down and steal a kiss before she had any idea what he was about. Confound it, he was fantasising about kissing the woman now! No, that was not what they were here for—why were they here, then? Ah, yes,

Emma, this was all about her—time he put all his energy into getting her what she wanted.

'Emma has always taken life too seriously, and her younger brother and sister take her sweet nature and patience with them for granted. When my cousin and his wife decided to send her here, I knew it was for the best because…but we both know this…' Harry stopped for a moment and struggled for words to describe the catastrophe that had engulfed the children's lives and his own. 'This disaster changes everything,' he managed to say at last and caught a flicker of sympathy in her cool blue eyes. They were more like the clear spring skies above them now—warm and worryingly inviting for a man who secretly needed comfort after such a cruel blow to the heart.

'Emma was beginning to blossom as her parents hoped, although I believe she missed her home more than she ever told them,' Miss Yelverton went on, as if she was weighing him up as guardian for children who had lost such excellent parents and finding him wanting.

Curse the wild reputation he had had so much fun earning, at first to goad his arctic father, but lately because he had felt oddly adrift after the old man died; wine, women and song had filled some of the gaps in his life until Christian and Jane died and left one nobody could cover. It wasn't as if he missed his father, but there was nobody left to infuriate, and that had been one certainty in his younger life—he could always rely on Sir Alfred Marbeck to be disgusted with his only child even when Harry did nothing wrong, so why not do it anyway? But never mind him now; as Harry doubted he was the right man to raise three lost and grieving children, he could hardly blame Miss Yelverton for doing so as well.

'My cousin and his wife put Emma's welfare before their own and miss her dreadfully,' he said half defensively, as if she was criticising Chris and Jane's painful decision to part with their beloved firstborn. Grief tugged at his composure as he heard himself use the present tense for people who were no longer present at all. 'They were the best people I have ever met, despite their peculiar idea of making me responsible for their children if anything happened to them.'

'Your task will be to prove them right, then, will it not?' she said, as if she thought it high time he lived up to Chris and Jane's excellent example.

She had steel of the right sort and the children needed some in their devastated lives. He could not play the stern parent. His father had been built from cold steel—might have been clamped together by nuts and bolts, for all his son knew—and Harry had sworn not to follow in his inflexible sire's footsteps at a very young age. He quite liked the idea of the old man rusting away now, instead of turning in his grave because Harry had been trusted with the care of his cousin's children when he should be the one who came to an untimely end, as the old man always predicted.

'I am hoping for your help with that tricky mission, Miss Yelverton,' he told her.

'*My* help? How on earth can *I* help you?' she asked, looking genuinely shocked.

'You are perfectly placed to become governess to my wards,' he forced himself to say blandly, as if it was an obvious solution, which it was; all he had to do now was make her believe it.

'What?' she asked, as if she could hardly believe her ears. 'Why on earth would I agree to be anything of the sort?'

At least she had not said *over my dead body*, but maybe that came next. 'I am sure Miss Thibett would have told me if you were deaf or short of understanding,' he could not resist saying because it seemed as if devils drove him at times, and even now they could not be silent. He thought for a moment she was about to forget her teacher's dignity and tell him exactly what she thought of him. It was there in her intriguing sky-blue eyes as they shot imaginary thunderbolts at him, and how could he have thought them warm and almost compassionate just now?

He should definitely walk away and leave her be; forget this whole ridiculous scheme to take on such a deliciously challenging female to teach his three little innocents, or one innocent and two enterprising little devils, if he was being strictly accurate. He shuddered at the idea of Lucy and Bram following in his footsteps one day, so he had to pull off what looked like a minor miracle now. Miss Yelverton was glaring at him as if she could not imagine how he had not been carted off to the local madhouse for the protection of the rest of humanity long ago.

'My apologies, ma'am; I let my tongue run away with me at times. It is a fault you should be eager to correct in my two younger wards before they learn from my bad example. To me, it sounds like a challenge to make a good teacher strain at the bit to start right away.'

'Oddly enough, it is not doing so for me,' she said severely.

Hmm, how was it even possible for such an attractive young woman not to know he enjoyed provoking her? He watched her clench her hands into fists behind her back in the reflection of the sparkling glass window to Miss Thibett's study behind her and wondered what that lady would make of such a giveaway gesture if she was looking up from her letters. Miss Yelverton's raised chin and clenched teeth said she was furious, even without the storm in her eyes he was glad only he could see. If she gave her true feelings away this easily, perhaps she was not the ideal governess after all, but Emma wanted her and that was that. Until Emma felt less devastated and steadier on her feet, it was his job to move heaven and earth to get Miss Yelverton to Chantry Old Hall with the rest of them.

'Then perhaps you should think again,' he told her. 'Emma loves you.' He paused to let that fact hit home. It seemed to be working because he saw her frown and then soften as she thought of the girl who must already have poured out her grief and devastation to the one person she was sure would listen to her. 'And I am always going to be a terrible example to a trio of innocents. Just imagine what their lives will be like if you do not agree to provide a better one for them to look up to.'

He should have left Emma's forlorn state to do its work with Miss Yelverton, because his genuine fear he might tow Chris's children's lives off course sounded facetious even to him. Curse the woman for making him feel such a fool he could not find the easy charm that usually got him what he wanted from females who ought to know better. Trust him to find the one who really did know better at exactly the wrong moment.

'Governesses are not antidotes for an employer's bad behaviour, Sir Henry,' she informed him snootily, then looked a little bit shocked by the fierce frown that hated form of his name brought on before he could order himself to stop it.

He relaxed his knitted brows with an effort of will and offered her an apologetic shrug instead. 'My late father was the only person who ever used that name for me,' he admitted gruffly. Surely even she would have heard of the bitter battles father and son fought as soon as Harry was big enough to shout back at the old windbag and defy every paternal order to simply do as he was bid and not argue.

'I am still not a bandage for hurts you need not cause in the first place. Your wards' well-being should be your main concern from now on, Sir Harry,' she told him severely.

He supposed he ought to be grateful she had modified his title to the one he answered to instead of the one he was christened with. 'Then do it because you love Emma. I know you must because she is a darling and has been ever since she opened her eyes on this bad old world of ours.'

He was challenging her to lie now and gave her a very direct look. He hoped she would read in it how dear Emma and the other two little monkeys were to him while she was staring back at him like a rabbit mesmerised by a fox. He was not given to showing his true feelings to anyone, let alone a complete stranger, so he hoped his wards would be grateful to him one day. No, he didn't. He never wanted the sort of guilt and grudge between him and his father to stand between him and Chris and Jane's children. He wanted the best for them and it was about time he charmed Miss Yelverton into giving it to them.

Chapter Two

Viola reminded herself she was a teacher and should be used to hanging on to her temper against the odds, but Sir Harry Marbeck added up to a lot more odds than a class full of restless schoolgirls. And he was quite right, drat the man. She did love Emma Marbeck and she was deeply concerned about the girl's future well-being, even before she had met her new guardian. Without the parents who loved her so much they sent her away for her own good, how could such a sweet-natured girl thrive in the kind of ménage Sir Harry Marbeck was sure to create around his three vulnerable wards? She shuddered to think of the rackety friends this man would invite into his home even with three young children in it.

And don't forget the loose women, Viola—apparently he specialised in encouraging them to be even looser than usual and enjoying all sorts of scandalous pastimes she did not even want to think about. Rumour said his latest mistress was the most sensuous beauty to light up the demi-monde in many a long year. Not that Miss Thibett encouraged rumours, but news of rakehells like Sir Harry Marbeck crept into the most unexceptional places and caused trouble. And this time he was here, doing it in person, and she was almost sure she wanted him to go away. Yes, she did; she wanted to go back to her peaceful and rewarding life here and forget all about him.

So Viola took a couple of deep breaths and hung on to her composure. Sir Harry Marbeck was even worse than rumour whispered. He was far more handsome, more dashing and much more danger-ously masculine than she let herself believe he could be when she heard the other teachers whispering and furtively giggling over his latest shocking misdeeds when Miss Thibett was not about to rebuke them.

She thought even then what a puzzle it was he managed to get away with them all without being excluded from polite society. Because he laughed with his eyes, she decided now she had actually met him—that was how he crept under a woman's best resolutions to resist him and chipped away at her composure until she only wanted to smile back at him like the village idiot.

Or at least that was how he had managed it with her. But, no, that was wrong—he had not managed it yet and, if she resisted this plan of his well enough, he never would. He was not going to bend her to the formidable will she sensed under all that raff-ish charm and get her under his roof to be made a mockery of by his wild and wicked friends. Wouldn't all those happily seduced mistresses he was credited with enjoying ever since he went up to Oxford laugh if they could see her playing the dowd in such exotic company?

'Fond though I am of Emma, I cannot risk my reputation and bring disgrace on my family by residing under your roof, Sir Harry,' she told him boldly because there was no point tiptoeing around the subject with a man who threatened to sweep her along in his wake like a force of nature.

'I will do anything it takes to help my late cousin's children feel safe and maybe even happy again one day, Miss Yelverton. I will even treat you as if you are old as the hills and ugly as sin if it will make you feel better, and I swear to you, hand on heart, I never seduce ladies of quality who do not want me to—especially ones who are under my roof to educate and look after my wards. You will have no need to fear for your reputation at my sooty hands.'

That was all he knew, she decided, as she forced back a sigh and a happy little simper at the very thought of feeling molten and eager under the sure touch of those hands and to hell with her virtue. She was human, for goodness' sake, and he was temptation incarnate; so many females had fallen for his careless charm and gilded good looks. It was the thought of an eager string of lovers lining up to be seduced by him that made her stiffen her backbone and resist this temptation to throw her bonnet over the windmill and go wherever he wanted her to.

'I could not live under your roof, Sir Harry,' she

told him as coolly as she had it in her to be when the very sight of him was heating up bits of her she had refused to allow to be heated during four weary years on the Dorset—then Bath—marriage circuit before she came here. 'Your intentions could be pure as driven snow towards me, but society would never believe it.'

'Am I really as bad as you paint me?' he asked with a frown that said he had no idea how tempting his golden looks and sleekly powerful masculine form were to the opposite sex.

He must be lying to himself about the potent spell he cast over even the most resistant female if he truly doubted it. Somehow that felt more dangerous than a cocky grin and a proud-of-himself shrug. No, she refused to be charmed into doing what he wanted despite her scruples.

'I suppose I must be if you have heard of my sins even under such a respectable roof as this. Confound them for getting in the way of the most sensible arrangements for the children's future I can think of, but nothing I say will undo them now,' he added, as if he was regretting being a pleasure-seeking gentleman of fabled good looks and excellent fortune just this once.

There was silence while they both thought about that very significant barrier to what she had to admit was a solution to Emma and her little brother and sister's immediate needs for their home and a good education. Viola remembered all too well how it felt to be lonely and apart from her own elder brother and sister. Her heart ached for the three much younger children who had been deprived of the love and security they had always known in one fell blow. They might be packed off to school or found a governess who would expect the children to behave like pattern cards or face a beating. At least she had been sixteen and still had her mother and father when Darius and Marianne left home to pursue love and life as older siblings must.

All the same, her memory of the gnawing loneliness she felt then whispered it was wrong of her to turn her back on Emma and two even younger children. It stopped her telling him an emphatic *No* and marching back inside to inform her headmistress of her decision. Instinct whispered he was uniquely dangerous to her and caution ordered her to leave a much more formidable lady to make it clear to him Miss Yelverton was not to be persuaded, so he might as well go away again.

'Would it be better if you and the children lived in their own home instead of my house?' He interrupted her thoughts as if he had been thinking up cunning ways to change her mind while she was busy resisting his appeal to her stupid senses. 'My formidable maiden aunt has moved into Chantry Old Hall in order to give the children her own peculiar version of comfort and daily irritation. If she was living at Garrard House as well, would that satisfy you I sincerely want the best for my wards? Her presence and a couple of miles of distance from my polluting company ought to silence any gossip, and I have already been wondering if the children would feel more settled in their own home rather than rattling about in mine.'

'I suggest you ask the lady if she is willing to disrupt her life again before you make fixed plans, but I suppose it might work,' she said doubtfully. She saw a flare of triumph in his bright blue eyes and, confound the man, he could see she was almost ready to agree to the impossible.

In the end, it was two weeks before Sir Harry Marbeck's messenger rode up to Miss Thibett's school with three missives, one addressed to Emma, one for Miss Thibett and another for Miss Yelverton. Secretly, Viola felt pleased at least one woman had held out against his strong will for so long. Miss Marbeck must have given in to him in the end, though, since Viola's letter was brief and businesslike and confirmed Sir Harry Marbeck's offer of the position of governess to his wards. How stupid of her to long for it to include something more personal than the list of conditions for her employment that he had now complied with, plus another of the ones he now expected her to agree to in her turn.

She must promise to stay at Garrard House for a period of no less than two years to provide the children with some much-needed stability. She had a month after commencing her employment to judge the strengths and weaknesses of each child and produce a plan for their education and a list of any extra lessons she thought they would need. She would be entitled to half a day off every week and two weeks' leave every year to allow her to visit family. He had named a very generous salary and informed Miss Yelverton she was not to argue, as, in view of the extra responsibility of overseeing the welfare and everyday lives of his wards, she would be earning every penny.

Ah, there was a touch of the personal among so much impersonal, then, and what a fool she was to cling to it like a shipwrecked mariner as the carriage made the final push up the wandering Cotswold road as they neared Garrard House and new lives for her and Emma. At least when they got there Emma forgot her sadness for a moment and gave a squeak of delight at the sight of her home—a fine, tall house built from local golden stone with tall sash windows designed to let in light and air as well as provide a splendid view. The house was set in wide gardens and the carriage had to wind up a neatly curved drive to get there, which made it clear to Viola that Mr Christian Marbeck must have been a rich man in his own right, as his cousin had inherited the grander family mansion even higher up in these hills. Garrard House commanded a magnificent view of the valley below and probably even over the top of the nearby hills so you could see beyond them to the Severn Plain from the windows of the main floor and above. It was no wonder that Emma loved the place, but Viola knew it must be bittersweet to come back without the hope of seeing her loving parents on the steps waiting to welcome her.

'Uncle Harry!' Emma shouted with enough excitement in her voice to banish the tears Viola had been anxiously watching gather as she wondered how on earth to distract the girl from this first sad homecoming.

And there he was, Sir Harry Marbeck, looking very different from the urbane and assured gentleman who made her heart skip like a dizzy fool back in Bath. This less contained and more vital-seeming Sir Harry was holding the dark-haired little girl clinging to his side like a monkey with one arm while a boy a couple of years older held his other hand and tried to pretend he was far too grown up to be openly delighted to see his big sister. Sir Harry's once immaculately arranged but now sun-lightened curls were ruffled by wind and little fingers and his neckcloth disarranged by the little girl's slightly grubby hands as she clung around his neck as if he was her rock in a stormy sea. He looked warm and human and far more magnificent than when he was in full fashionable fig and fine as fivepence. No wonder the littlest Marbeck was hanging on to him as if she never intended to let go while she sucked the thumb of her other hand and stared at the carriage with her big sister in it with wide dark eyes. There was something else there as well, a challenge, from the look of her stubbornly set mouth, for this governess lady she had been told was coming to teach her lessons she had no desire to learn.

'Oh, Uncle Harry! I am so pleased to see you,' Emma told him as she tumbled out of the carriage before anyone had time to step forward and pull down the steps or offer her a hand down.

'Welcome home, little love,' he said softly as Emma hurtled up the shallow wide steps to wrap her arms around his narrow waist and hug into him and all her family at once.

Somehow he managed to brace himself against the force of a half-grown girl throwing herself at him with such enthusiasm, keep the other girl safe and not let go of the boy. Viola watched with awe as this man she had told herself was a lightweight, who flitted through life charming everyone but never really meaning it, proved he was so much more. Damnation, now she would have to take him seriously and admit what a danger he posed her. She already longed to be part of that group as they stood there like a safe little unit that she had forced apart with her ridiculous scruples about living under the same roof as a rake. Oh, curse it—she should never have come here. Should never have signed that promise to stay two years; never have blithely accepted his more than generous terms of employment.

Now she was regretting being so wilfully blind to his potent masculine appeal and her own weakness before she had even stepped down from the luxury of his fine carriage. She was already counting this off as her first day towards freedom and safety, and what a beginning this was for her new life as a governess. She steeled herself to step down in a far more collected manner than her eldest pupil and plastered a cool smile on her face as she met Sir Harry's rueful gaze.

'Welcome to Garrard House, Miss Yelverton,' he said, as if this was just one more day, and he was right, wasn't he? For him it obviously was. 'This little minx is Lucy and this young gentleman is Master Bramford Marbeck. I hope you are going to make your best bow to Miss Yelverton, Bram, since I cannot quite manage one at the moment and one of us ought to bid a lady welcome in form.'

The boy did so without letting go of the man's hand, and that was when Viola had to acknowledge the love between these children and their unlikely guardian was not born of guilt on his part and need on theirs—it was a custom long established between them. He must have been an important part of their childhood to have their love and confidence, and he had probably been their beloved Uncle Harry since they were old enough to be aware they had one. Now the wretched man was forcing her to see the deep feelings he tried to hide from the wider world when she had been trying to fool herself all the way here that he had none.

She had told herself she was safe as a marble statue in his dangerous company, for all the appeal he could have to her well-guarded heart. The danger of him doing any damage to it had made her form a paper version of him in her head after he left Bath to persuade Miss Marbeck to move down here and live with her great-nephew and great-nieces so that their new governess need not fear for her good name under Sir Harry's roof. Now that the real man was standing here with his three adored wards unmistakably adoring him right back, the paper version was no more than a few tatters on the wind. Miss Viola Yelverton was in deep trouble over a man who would never want her back.

Dignity, Viola, she ordered herself as she dipped him a half-hearted curtsy in reply to his welcome and gave Bram a more sincere one as she met the little imp's eyes with a rueful look. Lucy was glaring at her new governess as she held fast to her beloved Uncle Harry—as if she thought Viola a rival for his affections. The little girl would soon find out her mistake, and Viola stepped forward as a lady with iron-grey hair and steely eyes stepped out of the front door and fixed Viola with a gimlet gaze.

At least there were going to be plenty of challenges in her new life to take her mind off the master of Chantry Old Hall—a place Viola sincerely hoped was a lot further away than the couple of miles Emma had told her about on the way here.

Chapter Three

August 1814

'Good afternoon, Miss Yelverton,' Sir Harry said from the doorway of the sunny sitting room at Garrard House where Viola was writing to her sister.

Somehow she managed not to jump, but why had her senses not prickled to warn her he was near so she could put up all her barriers in time? *Better erect them now, then*, she told herself bracingly. She took a long, slow breath to ward off the stupid feeling of breathless delight that always threatened to overwhelm her when he was nearby, however hard she told it not to. 'Good afternoon, Sir Harry,' she replied and wished her heart would stop pounding like one of his precious racehorses at the gallop. She laid down her pen and watched him as if he had interrupted a vital task and she was impatient to get back to it.

'I had a letter from Lucy,' he explained. 'Inviting me to nursery tea,' he went on with a slight frown, as if he was wondering why she was down here in the middle of an afternoon instead of upstairs with her pupils.

'I see,' Viola said limply and wished he was the sort of guardian who ignored messages from his wards.

'I cannot disappoint a lady,' he said and frowned further at her carefully blank expression, indicating that perhaps those words did not sound quite right to him either.

'Of course not,' she said, and the spectre of all the ladies he had not disappointed ran through her head like a bevy of ghostly beauties wearing smug smiles and whispering *He wanted us, but he will never want a drab little mouse like you*, but she already knew that.

'Especially a very young lady whom I love,' he added almost defiantly, as if he could see those ghosts as well.

'Your aunt has taken Bram and Emma to visit Bram's godmother, and she asked me to leave Lucy alone upstairs to have a good hard think about her appalling conduct last time she went there.'

'Oh…lud,' Sir Harry replied so slowly that Viola mentally filled in the gaps since she had a soldier brother and her own childhood as a tomboy to supply plenty of oaths a true lady would not know; one more thing to shock him about the real woman under the prim exterior if he ever bothered to look. 'It's no wonder Aunt Tam refused to take Lucy, after the fuss she caused last time,' he added ruefully.

'Miss Marbeck told me how forthright Lucy was about Lady Lubley's wig and lapdogs last time.'

'She is a stubborn little monkey and I have no idea how she thought she was going to get away with her martyr act. Everyone must know she has been left behind as a punishment and someone was sure to tell me.'

'I know Lucy has a hot temper and plenty of devilment, but she *is* only six and a half, Sir Harry. Luckily she is not awake on every suit yet.'

'She will be dangerous when she is.'

'And it is my lot to teach her not to hurt and manipulate people for her own ends before she gets that far.'

'Not a task I envy you, Miss Yelverton,' he told her with a smile that did unfair things to her insides. 'And I cannot see her regretting her sins when she has been spared a trip to Lubley Lodge to apologise for them either.'

'Being left upstairs alone to think about her sins *is* a punishment.'

'Have you met Lady Lubley, Miss Yelverton?' he asked with such humour in his eyes she had to force herself not to smile fatuously back at him and agree with every word he said.

'No, but Lucy was very rude to her great-aunt as well as to Her Ladyship, and please do not tell me Lucy is too young to know what she was saying when we both know differently. Whatever Lady Lubley said or did, Miss Marbeck does not deserve to be shouted at by a little girl in a temper tantrum.'

'Lucy was an infernal brat and made it worse by refusing to say she was sorry afterwards. She made Aunt Tam ashamed of helping raise such a forthright little madam, and I have never seen my stalwart aunt as low as when she told me exactly what the little imp said and did that day.'

'She was too busy being furious with her for being so rude and unrepentant to let me see that,' Viola said.

'Don't forget I have known my aunt a lot longer than you have,' he said, as if she needed comforting because Miss Marbeck had not confided her true feelings in a governess when she thought they were almost friends after a year and a half living in the same house.

'Of course she would confide her worries to you, Sir Harry. You are Miss Marbeck's nephew as well as the children's guardian.'

'I would have thought that was a drawback rather than an asset,' he said. No wonder he was determined the children would know they were loved, if he was unsure his aunt loved him even now. Viola wondered at the stiffness and lack of heart in Sir Harry's own childhood for him to doubt it, but told herself it was none of her business and neither was he.

'I do remember how grim it felt to be dressed up and told to be on my best behaviour, then taken on visits to crotchety elderly relatives as a boy, though,' he went on as blithely as if he had no idea the thought of him as a wary and perhaps unloved child might melt her heart if she was not very careful. He was certainly not vulnerable and unloved now.

'So do I—indeed, I expect most people can if they are being honest,' she replied, feeling a little bit guilty because she could never be truly honest with him for the sake of her peace of mind as well as his and that wretched contract she had signed not to leave for another six months.

'As her guardian, I have to be horrified by Lucy's misdeeds, but I will admit only to you, Miss Yelverton, the scrubby schoolboy in me sneakily admires her for saying things I longed to back then, but never quite dared.'

'We had to learn not to be rude to our elders and so must she,' Viola said. A stubborn shimmer of wicked excitement was humming away deep inside her at the thought he was telling her something he had confided in nobody else and that simply would not do. She could not allow herself to be charmed into sympathy with Lucy's boredom and frustration. She could not let him see he could beguile her into letting the little minx off her sins if he tried only a little harder.

'We all want her to learn some manners, although I admit I am surprised Bram and Emma did not join in,' he went on, as oblivious to her needy inner woman as ever. 'I would have, or at least I would if there was a chance of escaping a thrashing when my father got me home and if I hadn't known he would keep me on bread and water for a month to teach me not to embarrass him in public ever again.'

Sir Alfred Marbeck must have been a harsh par-

ent, but she had to forget the vulnerable boy this potent man grew out of or risk revealing far too much.
'I am governess to your wards, Sir Harry,' she reminded him. 'When they are rude I get the blame
for not correcting them sternly enough. It could spoil
my chances of finding a good position when I leave.'

'A very good reason why you must stay here, then,
although I doubt you are hard hearted enough to leave
my aunt to cope with the little devils on her own.
After all, what use would I be in helping her to correct a lack of good manners when I have so few myself?' He asked as if he really was a light-minded
fribble and she should not care enough to feel cross
about it. 'I know my cousin indulged his youngest
child and I also know Lucy needs to learn manners
and some consideration for the feelings of others before she becomes an insufferable brat. Until now I
was too worried about her happiness to worry over-
much how her mischief could affect others, but I can
see I was wrong to put that before everything and
carry on spoiling her.'

'I am glad you realise it now, but your neighbours
will still say you should find a more experienced
governess or send the children to school if you truly
want them to learn better manners.' She wanted him
to send her away before she did or said something
that could not be undone. Yet it would be such a
wrench to go.

It hurt to feel; she should have stayed at Miss Thibett's, where she could care about her pupils enough
to want them to do their best in the next class up, but

not feel as if part of her heart was being ripped out when they moved on. She refused to even think about the gap never seeing him again was going to leave as he went on as if he had no idea how she felt. But how could he? Because he was a man and a self-assured and handsome one as well, so of course he did not.

'Not if they want to remain on good terms with me they will not,' he said. 'You know I cannot send them away when they are still grieving for their parents. Your kindness to all three of my wards is too important for me to replace you with a stern harridan simply to keep the Lady Lubleys of this world happy, Miss Yelverton.'

'Thank you for your forbearance, Sir Harry,' Viola said limply and tried to mean it.

'It is not forbearance. It's terror,' Harry admitted, shocked by the realisation that a hole threatened to open up in his life if Miss Yelverton left here as she seemed to want to. 'The children would be bereft if you returned to Miss Thibett's school, so I cannot afford to lose you and neither can they. Since she is the adult in this drama and Lucy is a small girl, Lady Lubley comes out of this far worse than a six-year-old with a hasty temper. She cannot expect three grieving children to behave like pattern cards in her tedious presence; I know I itch to be off after five minutes of her company.'

'Lucy might grow up as demanding and difficult as Lady Lubley if she does not learn to be kinder as well as more polite.'

It was a horrible thought, but he refused to countenance it. 'And losing you would make her worse and unsettle all three of my wards and their great-aunt as well. You seem to be fated to remain here until the children are full grown, Miss Yelverton, since clearly none of us can manage without you,' he said all too truthfully and fought down a sense of panic at the very notion of doing so.

He had been a good baronet; he had stayed away from Garrard House as much as he could without making the children feel he did not love them any more. He kept a mistress in luxury nearby to sate this ridiculous need for a woman he could not have. He shifted uncomfortably even now because somehow he still wanted Miss Yelverton anyway, but that was his own particular hair shirt to wear and his duty to make sure she never found out about it.

'Your wards might be better off with children of their own age,' she argued. Why on earth would she not let the idea go and leave him to find Lucy so he could make it clear to her she was being a brat?

'As you have just pointed out to me, Lucy is only six and a half years old, and even Emma is not twelve for a few months. We have years before decisions about their schooling need to be made, and you are doing an excellent job in the meanwhile.'

'Boys often go to preparatory schools at seven and Bram is eight,' she persisted, and he could hardly shake her for it when that would make matters even worse.

'School can wait until he is ready, or he can stay until he is at Oxford, as far as I am concerned,' he said with what he thought was exemplary patience under the circumstances.

'He will want to get away from his sisters long before that. He needs friends of his own age and a fair share of boyish adventures before he must take care of his sisters and this house and land when he comes of age.'

'That is my worry, not his,' Harry said with a frown. 'Chris's will left me responsible for Bram's inheritance until he is five and twenty and Lucy and Emma are the same age or married. I must talk to him about the terms of his parents' wills if he is worrying about this house and his sisters' future instead of catching frogs and climbing trees and doing all the things grubby boys should at his age. At least I will have plenty of time to work my way into the role of stern guardian to the girls. By the time Emma makes her debut, I should be ready to glower at her suitors like a tyrant in a play,' he said lightly enough, but even by then he could not imagine this place without Miss Yelverton looking on as if she disapproved of their guardian, but secretly doted on his wards.

'And even when she is old enough to make her come out, Emma will need help and encouragement, Sir Harry,' she warned him, but didn't she know he worried enough about Emma without her assistance? 'You were quite right to remove her from Miss Thibett's school until she could recover from the first shock of her loss, but it might be best if she went back before too long. She should not worry about a little brother and sister all the time, and she needs friends of her own age so she will not feel lonely and lost when she makes her curtsy to polite society.'

'Is that how *you* felt, then?' he demanded rudely. Being curious about her helped to salve this raw feeling inside because she would not stop pushing him to send the children to school, presumably so she could go back to the delights of teaching at Miss Thibett's Academy for Young Ladies. Did she have a beau in Bath who had agreed to be left behind so they could save up to be wed all the sooner, then? Jealousy at the thought of her pining for her poor and passionate suitor raged through him like an artillery barrage at the very thought of the man even as he decided that, no, no sane man could endure watching his love leave a safe and respectable post to work for the likes of him.

No beau, then… So, why was she in such a hurry to get back to the drudgery of teaching a whole classroom full of girls instead of his delightful two and Bram? He paid her well, and goodness knew it had taken him every promise and incentive he had to persuade Aunt Tam to come here and make all respectable in the first place. What on earth ailed the woman that she was nearly begging him to let her go now?

'I felt…'

What a question to ask her and how on earth was she supposed to answer it when even she did not know quite how to describe her feelings at the time of her own come out?

'I was in a very different situation to the one

Emma will face when she is old enough to make her debut,' she said and hoped he would let the matter of hers drop.

'You were still a young woman on the verge of adulthood, with all the thrills and pitfalls of life waiting for you,' he insisted, as if he really wanted to know how she had felt and what she had wondered about as a girl, as if he was thinking of her as someone more than just a governess. Why must he poke about in her head when she still felt tender and raw about the whole wretched business of her debut? She had enough to endure with him close enough to touch, and why did she have to feel like this about him anyway? None of her suitors back then had made her want to be siren-like and sensual so she could make them want her as surely as she wanted him.

'I am a vicar's daughter, Sir Harry, not a minor heiress in my own right like Emma and Lucy,' she said brusquely to discourage him from asking her anything else and encourage him to go away again.

'That made you less subject to the pitfalls and triumphs of the social world, did it? I think not, Miss Yelverton,' he said, as if she had piqued his interest and he refused to let the subject drop.

'Of course not,' she said with a defensive glare to say she was not happy with this topic and it was time he amused himself elsewhere.

'Then what was it like? As I have never been a genteel young lady, I have no idea how it feels to be one. I want to understand what Emma needs to do before she gets there and it is too late to prepare her for the pitfalls of polite society.'

'It will not be too late for her,' Viola said. Emma would have him in the background, always concerned, forever on the watch for wolves and ready to head them off before they could do his beloved ward harm. 'She will have you,' she felt driven to explain, because he truly did care and that made him even more of a temptation.

'Not many respectable people would think me an asset as guardian and protector. I always thought you were one of the front runners in the race to find me wanting, Miss Yelverton.'

Did he sound a little bit hurt by the idea she disapproved of him? Even if he was, it would be a fleeting wince. 'Set a rake to catch a rake,' she said carelessly, and his sudden frown said how little he liked her lazy analogy.

Chapter Four

'What a very high opinion of me you do have,' he said. She wanted him to be cool and on his way to somewhere else, so she should have been happy when he turned away, as if he had wasted enough breath on her today.

Instead she felt bereft and contrary and confused when she ought to be congratulating herself he had no idea she ached for his touch on her hand or just a brief meeting of eyes—anything rather than their usual avoidance of one another and awkwardness when they really had to talk. A kiss was a bad idea, even if he would not find the idea of kissing the children's governess wrong and ridiculous. Imagining his firm mouth teasing and tempting on hers was pure folly and she had to stop it this minute. What were they talking about? Ah, yes, Emma and her guardian in the far-off future. She seized on the idea and at least she could let a little bit of her feelings out without him noticing that way.

'No, that's not what I meant to say at all. I was going to tell you that Emma will never need to puzzle her way around flattery and clever words with you there to make it plain to any liars and opportunists to look elsewhere at the double or risk your fury,' she explained because she was too weak to want him to go away with such an unfavourable opinion of her, or to go away at all, if it came to the exact truth of the matter.

'Is that what you had to endure?' he turned back to ask her, as if he really wanted to know, and how dare he be so perceptive when she did not want him to know about those years of slights and whispers and not very well-hidden mockery.

'Of course not; I am only a vicar's daughter, Sir Harry,' she said, and the misery of years in the drawing rooms and ballrooms of the minor gentry felt bitter all over again. 'I have little money and a scholarly father not as strong as we would all like him to be, and not many young men can afford to marry solely for love, even if they wanted to.'

'You must have met one or two who could. Even at country balls and house parties, there would be some with means to afford a wife with a small dowry.'

'You have no idea how it feels to be continuously pushed at such gentlemen, Sir Harry,' she said, remembering the shame and frustration roused in her when her mother had done so and refused to listen to Viola's bitter protests. 'You are a man, for one thing, and a powerful and wealthy one for two more, so how could you know what it feels like to be branded a husband hunter? I am not sure if my mother's desperation to get one of her daughters married respectably hurt her or me the most, since I hated the whole wretched business and came to dislike her in the doing of it as well.

'It is mortifying to become a person you do not want to be, Sir Harry. In the end, I hated being primped and polished for the marriage mart so much I begrudged every penny my mother spent on our appearances as she trundled me around every party or soirée or subscription ball she could contrive an invitation to, first while we lived in Dorset, and then in Bath after my father retired there because of ill health.'

'You must have had offers,' he said, and she supposed she should be flattered that he thought so.

'Oh, yes, and some of them were even respectable. My mother was delighted until I turned them all down.'

'Why?'

Why? How could he even ask her such a question?

She turned away to stare sightlessly out of the generous window at the sunny gardens below. *Because I never felt a hint of the heat and edgy delight I feel at being even this close to you* was the true answer, of course. The one she hit on instead was how destroying it felt to be reduced to an object for sale to the highest bidder. 'I felt nothing for any of the gentlemen in question,' she replied at last. 'I might have settled for friendship and respect, but how could I respect a man my mother cozened into thinking I would be a quiet and biddable wife? I could not even like the ones who offered marriage when I would not take their less respectable offers and I almost forgot the one who thought he should try a yellow-headed chit since his last two wives were dark.'

'Fool,' Harry said scornfully.

She almost smiled because he was quite right. 'Yes, he was,' she agreed with a sigh. 'But dowerless girls attract fools and satyrs. Emma will be much luckier, and since you will never allow her to be pushed into marriage or preyed on by fortune hunters, I have no idea why you are worrying. She has years to go before there is any need to be concerned about her finding her feet among her own kind.'

'It sounds as if I have every need to worry,' he said with concern in his blue eyes that said he had read between the lines of her own tale of life as a dowerless girl in a commercial world and he might pity her if she was not careful. 'Knowing how sternly independent you are, your mother's desire to marry you off must have made life very hard for you at times.'

Only at times, Sir Harry? she thought bitterly. She had not even told him about having to dodge advances that certainly did not involve marriage, or the near rape only a handy candlestick over the man's head had averted. Or her hurt and shame when she had overheard a young man she almost believed she could marry confide in his friends he was only having a bit of fun before he settled down with the girl his family actually wanted him to marry. It was a puzzle even to her why the slights and disappointments of that time still felt raw and dark even now, like an open graze that had never healed. Pride, she told herself wearily, and what a prickly bedfellow it was. Now Sir Harry knew about those days, perhaps he would leave her be. Yet he was still standing by the desk where she had been sitting writing before he came in, as if he was trying to see the real Miss Viola Yelverton behind an averted face and closed expression.

'At least I learned to be very careful what I said and did back then. It has stood me in good stead as a teacher,' she said as lightly as she could manage to fill the silence as he let it stretch. It felt best to fill it with something. If not, she might forget herself completely and plead with him to understand how much she hurt during those long, lonely years when Marianne and Darius had gone and nobody else seemed to want to understand her. 'And luckily for me my father believed me when I told him I was at the end of my tether with the whole wretched business and would rather hire myself out as a housemaid than endure one more Season on the marriage mart. So you see, Sir Harry, mine is a mundane tale and can tell you nothing about how life will be for your wards when they are old enough to be presented at court.'

'It tells me a great deal about you, Miss Yelverton,' he said softly, and there was something in his eyes that made her heart race even as her well-honed instincts stepped back in horror. 'It makes me wonder if maybe you wear nothing-coloured gowns and a ridiculous cap as a disguise.'

Thank heavens he had not seen her as husband-hunting Miss Yelverton with her gowns always cut a little too low for strict propriety on her mama's orders and her hair primped into artful disorder to make her look even more available. The very idea made her shudder and be grateful for her nothing-coloured gown and the cap he thought so ridiculous. 'Governesses must keep up a respectable appearance,' she told him with a shudder for how vulnerable she had felt on all the fringes of society.

'Not as respectable as that,' he argued with a nod at her buff-coloured gown as if it was a personal offence. 'I wager you retreated behind it the day you became Miss Thibett's junior teacher instead of Mrs Yelverton's most rebellious daughter.'

'You have not met the other one,' she argued with an almost smile, conjuring the image of Marianne dancing off to marry her soldier, never mind what anyone said to the contrary. 'I did not retreat behind it,' she argued, then blushed because he was right. 'And what does it matter if I did?'

'I hate waste,' he said, as if that explained everything.

'It is not waste. You are the one who persuaded me that Emma and her brother and sister needed me when we were back in Bath, so who I am now matters far more than who I might have been once upon a time. I need to look the plain and upright governess under your roof to counter any rumours that might have followed me from my other life.'

'As this is not my roof, don't try to use it to get

me off the subject. Your retreat from the world could leave the girls with a skewed view of how life is for a young woman, so maybe you ought to join in with the family now and again when Aunt Tam asks you to, instead of citing your position as an excuse to hide yourself away like a nun. If you want them to be relaxed about the prospect of womanhood and feel comfortable in their own shoes, would it hurt you to be sociable now and again?'

'Probably not,' she said with a shrug so he would not know it might.

'Then I shall expect you to join Aunt Tam and the children next time they come to Chantry Old Hall to invade my kitchens and inspect the still room and generally turn the whole place upside down.'

'Very well; is that all for now, then, Sir Harry?' she asked with a bland, blank stare to say he was in the way and she wanted to finish her letter to her sister before her unexpected afternoon of leisure came to an end.

'I think it is probably enough,' he said with a smile that did wicked things to her insides again.

More than enough, she silently challenged him. He had won again. It felt as if she had shown him things she did not want anyone else to know about, while he stood there as if he had no idea how much it had cost her to admit to such a humiliating and unattractive past.

'As I am here, I might as well go up and see Lucy—next time she might truly need me and she must know that I will always come.'

'You are as soft as butter with all three of your wards,' Viola accused and heard a fond exasperation in her own voice she hoped he had not noticed. 'Lucy is still naughty, and her brother and sister had to endure another duty visit despite being good last time and that is not fair,' she told him sharply to cover it up. 'If Lucy gets away with this, they might imitate her next time and get a bad name as ungovernable brats responsible for the mischief for miles around.'

'Heaven forbid,' Sir Harry said with a visible shudder. 'I can hardly imagine Emma being an infernal brat, but even the thought of Bram being wicked as well is enough to bring even me out in hives. You have made your point, then, ma'am,' he said. At least this time he went away with a polite half-bow in her direction and a sad shake of his head at the very idea.

Harry ran upstairs towards the sunny nurseries at the top of what he still thought of as Christian and Jane's house, although it was Bram's now. He paused on the half-landing to stare at the glorious view of the valley from the tall windows his cousin had put in to light the staircase and reveal the Cotswold Hills spread out like a bed full of lovers asleep under a patchwork of greens and gold. He tried to appreciate it as it deserved, but could not get Miss Yelverton's story out of his head. She had a bad habit of being in there far more often than a governess should be, and lately she had started to tease his senses and intrigue him at all the wrong moments. Well, if he was being strictly honest, she had done that from the first moment he laid eyes on her in Miss Thibett's neatly respectable garden.

Now that Miss Yelverton had finally allowed him a glimpse of the woman beneath the dull-coloured gowns and unadorned spinster caps, he felt even more teased and intrigued. If she had only cast out silken lures and flirted with her eyes from beneath the delicious sweep of her curling gold-tipped lashes, he could have run in the opposite direction, but, despite that sad tale of her life as a poverty-stricken husband hunter, there was still an innocence about her that said, no, it was simply not her style to simper or sigh her way to a rich husband and secure future.

In truth, his heart went out to the very young and far less defended Miss Yelverton he could see behind the woman she thought she was now. It almost made it worse when the voice of reason said her mother was quite right to try to establish her daughter well. Most of the aristocracy and gentry married for commercial reasons with a light veneer of romance. He was lucky that Bram's existence spared him from making such a marriage. In exchange for his title and lands, he would have to ask for the promise of an heir and condemn himself to a lifetime of pretending Lady Marbeck was all he had ever longed for in a woman. The very idea made him shudder.

That said, he recalled Christian courting Jane and their secret smiles and furtive little touches which said they could not keep their eyes off one another. Nobody could accuse them of making a dynastic marriage or being less than deeply in love with one another from that time until the day they died together in that appalling, senseless accident. No, they were a blissfully happy exception; his parents' marriage, on the other hand, proved what happened when a couple had not a shred of love to share between them, not even enough for the product of their ill-advised union.

He had learned very young that marriage was a curse to be avoided at all costs and he supposed that made Miss Yelverton his soulmate in an odd way. They were both wary and battle-scarred by the marriage customs of their kind. Knowing she hurt under that front of serene indifference to the eyes of the world ought to make him forget his urgent need for the woman in his bed. Yet he did want her to know he did not think any less of her for escaping the life her mother had laid out for her.

A goodly part of him wanted to take his wards' governess in his arms and let her weep out the hurt and loneliness he heard in her voice as she described that time, as if he had forced the words out of her. He hated himself for doing it, yet he felt triumphant that she had let him see the woman under the cool disguise. Devil take it, the woman had him so confused he didn't know what he wanted. He felt torn by so many contrary feelings it was as if she was half a dozen women at the same time, all of them complex and contradictory.

And it had to stop; he reminded himself he never meant to marry and Miss Yelverton was not a young woman he could trifle with and move on. They would have to wed, and the blight of his parents' marriage had settled on him too young to make it credible Sir Harry would ever love and adore a Lady Marbeck of his own. His mother departed when Harry was five years old, so he barely remembered her. Fifteen years older than Harry, it was his cousin Chris who made sure Harry was fed, amused and educated after Harry's mother left.

He stared down at this view Chris had loved so much and missed his cousin and Jane so fiercely it hurt. Garrard House was only open because of Miss Yelverton and his own wild reputation. It was his grand sacrifice for his wards' sake—a burr in his stockings he could never quite forget while he was living in his grand house two miles away. If only she was as plain and invisible as she thought, his life would be much easier.

'But still, confound the woman for being who she is instead of who she thinks she is,' he muttered very softly. Somehow he would pretend he was as indifferent to her as she was to him. Now he came to think about it, that was odd. She was warm and natural with the children and Aunt Tam, and the servants liked her, so she could not be stiff and cold with them. Why was he the only one she watched as if he might turn and bite her? He had never tried to flirt with her or followed this feral tug of attraction to its logical conclusion by trying to bed her. Was it an old habit of brushing off any slightly eligible male before he could get any wrong-headed ideas about wanting to marry her? She *had* fended him off as if he was poisonous. Best not wonder any more in case he got overexcited and ran back down to try kissing her until their eyes crossed and they forgot to wonder why not.

'Why are you standing there, Uncle Harry? I'm hungry.' Lucy's voice interrupted his thoughts and he gave her a warm smile she did not deserve.

'You are always in a hurry for the next thing, my Lucy,' he said.

'Hurrying is the best way to get there.'

'Hmm, but what a shame you are not as eager to be good. Why did I only just find out your Great-Aunt Tamara has gone to Lubley Lodge with your brother and sister to apologise for your bad behaviour again? You are meant to be thinking about your rudeness and it makes me sad to know you cannot be trusted. I have wasted a ride over here on a hot afternoon.'

'Why?' Lucy said with her head on one side to let him see what a charming child she was and how harshly she had been judged.

'I do not eat or drink with cheats or dissemblers,' he told her with a stern look. Miss Yelverton was right to worry—the little terror would become more and more of a handful if she was not checked.

'What's a dismemberer, Uncle Harry?' Lucy said with a genuinely puzzled frown.

He had to bite back a bark of laughter at her mistake, but best not answer that question and risk giving her nightmares. 'A dissembler is a clever liar, Lucy, and I fear that word fits you all too well. After I had told everyone my Lucy would never be deliberately cruel or lie to get her own way as well. I did not want to believe you had been so rude to a lady your parents chose to be Bram's godmother.' *For some odd reason that has always escaped me*, he added in the privacy of his own head.

'She said I am a fidget and Aunt Tam was a fool to take me to see her since I am obviously too young and silly to know how to behave myself in polite company,' Lucy said sulkily.

'And after your great-aunt gave you the benefit of the doubt by taking you there as well?'

'There you are, then. You agree with me.'

'No, that I do not,' he almost shouted, then hastily got his temper back under control. He could hear his father's cold fury in his own voice and it horrified him. Now he only had to swallow a sick feeling at the very idea he could take after the man he spent most of his life trying not to follow in any way but the obvious one and he would be himself again. He refused to lose his temper with Chris's children, especially this one.

Lucy was too young to have strong memories of their parents, and that was going to be a lifelong sadness for both of them. 'A careless comment by a lonely old lady should not make you behave badly, Lucy. Now you have tried to get around your punishment for doing so by inviting me here when you knew you could not leave the nursery. I am hurt that you tried to use me in such a sly way. Do I always have to doubt your word from now on?' he asked.

'This is our house, not Aunt Tam's, or Miss Yelverton's, or yours. It's my home, so I can do what I like in it,' Lucy raged, as if being found out had fuelled her fury. Temper tears shone in the dark eyes she'd inherited from her father, but there was something deeper and more difficult to cope with behind them. Harry felt stupid with the apprehension that he would not find the right things to say if that something broke free and landed them both in the suds.

'You can stop that nonsense, young lady,' he said clumsily, praying for inspiration when he had not even known he could. 'You are six years old, not a grown-up lady like Miss Yelverton and your Great-Aunt Tamara, and even if you were a royal princess, you would have to do as you are bid until you are many years older and wiser than you are now, and never mind who owns what.'

Lucy screwed up her face and got ready to wail and stamp her feet at being thwarted, and Harry felt his ears starting to hurt in anticipation.

'You deserved every word of Sir Harry's rebuke, Lucy Marbeck, so stop it right now, unless you would like to go to bed right away and stop there without any supper,' Miss Yelverton told her youngest pupil as she ran up the stairs to find out what the noise was.

Harry wanted to kiss her feet for interrupting, but instead smiled sheepishly and shrugged to admit she was a lot better at this than he was. She looked warm and a little bit flustered after climbing two flights of stairs in such a hurry, and he felt a flip of need in his belly. It threatened to turn rampant as he eyed her parted lips and slightly quickened breath and wanted everything he could not have. *Fool*, he chided himself and concentrated on watching Lucy instead. Her tears had dried up so rapidly he realised she must be able to turn them on and off at will. He was secretly impressed by her acting and a lot warier about falling for it in future.

'I dare say if you behave yourself for the next week Sir Harry will come to tea with you and your brother and sister at the end of it. If you are not too busy, of course, Sir Harry?'

'If you can manage the gargantuan effort of behaving yourself for such a long time I will be so impressed I shall invite all three of you to take it with me at Chantry Old Hall, as well as Miss Yelverton and your Great-Aunt Tam,' Harry told Lucy. He managed to hide his smile as he watched her measure the effort that would cost her against the allure of being spoilt by his cook and most of his staff for a whole afternoon.

'What's gar...gargantuan?' she asked warily.

'It means making a huge effort, a giant labour.' Just like the one he was making not to burst out laughing at her mangling of the word. Miss Yelverton's carefully blank expression told him she was having the same problem, and there he was, back admiring her far more than he ought to and wanting to kiss her far too much for his comfort and her propriety.

'It will be very hard,' Lucy said with a heavy sigh. Again he wanted to laugh, but she would be insulted, and, naughty or not, he did not want her hurt. 'But not impossible?' he asked seriously.

'No,' she admitted at last.

'Then I shall send the barouche next Saturday. I hope you will be free to join us, Miss Yelverton?' he said—why the deuce had he invited her as well? The children could have come up to Chantry Old Hall with Aunt Tam and the nursery maid or their old nanny. Then he would not have to spend the afternoon pretending he was not in the least bit fascinated by a governess who did not want him. Although he might cherish a fantasy of her being warm and sharing laughter with him instead of her best impression of a clockwork governess, it was only an air dream. He had never been the kind of rogue who seduced respectable young women doing their best to earn an honest living, and he was certainly not going to start with her.

'Thank you, Sir Harry,' she replied blandly. He must have imagined the flash of panic in her eyes before she lowered them so he could only see the top of the spinster's cap she deluded herself hid the beauty of her sky-blue eyes and the odd wisp of moonbeams-and-starlight hair from lecherous fools like him, when in fact it only made things worse.

'Good, then that is settled,' he said too heartily. 'And now I have unfinished business at my Home Farm I would be glad to resolve, if you two ladies will excuse me?' he added cravenly.

Miss Yelverton's cool *Of course* overrode Lucy's

No and he chose to listen to the governess. He left them behind with a sigh of relief he only just managed to keep inside until he was out of earshot.

Chapter Five

At last Harry was outside again in the summer sun and on his way to the stables to retrieve his favourite mount from a cool interlude and some pampering from the bored groom now only responsible for the children's ponies and a stolid old hack of Aunt Tam's.

It suddenly occurred to him that Miss Yelverton ought to have a suitable horse to ride. First he must find out if she could ride, of course, or if it would be best to let her learn on Emma's fat pony until she was ready for a docile mare of her own. No, the whole idea was impossible. He did not trust himself to teach her to ride and hated the thought of a groom laying hands on her slender waist to steady her when she was in danger of falling off. There might be all sorts of touching and fumbling and lusting after the exquisite body under all that dour clothing that she thought made her invisible to the male of the species. *Wrong, Miss Yelverton, so wrong I wonder you even think it might.*

What the devil was her name? He ought to have a more intimate way to think about the feminine thorn in his side. Maybe it was a plain kind of name, the sort she looked as if she wanted to own up to. Perhaps she was a Mary or a Jane or an Ann? Or a fair Rosamund or sweet Charity, or a fine and queenly Isabella, he thought ruefully as he waited impatiently for the groom to saddle his own fidgety gelding. Given how stupidly he lusted after her, maybe she was a Morgana or even Guinevere. He grinned at the idea of a respectable vicar and his wife naming one of their brood after such a witchy female. Curse it, here he was, obsessing about the woman all over again.

He had plenty of society flirts who were well up to snuff and would not take a light-hearted flirtation for anything more. And Gloriana lived on the other side of the park, always ready, willing and able to distract him from cool-eyed and unavailable governesses. Except somehow he never quite managed to want his mistress as much as Miss Yelverton, who would probably freeze him with icy indifference if he was villain enough to try to seduce a lady under his protection in a very different sense of the word.

Now he was fixed in the countryside for the foreseeable future, Glory was restless for the sophisticated delights of London and Brighton. If he was a better man, he would pay her off and let her find a protector less tied to his ancestral home. But if Glory left him, he would be frustrated and might dream of the unattainable governess every night. Another puzzle he was trying not to work to a logical conclusion.

He managed a cheerful *Thank you* and *Good day* for the groom and cursed his own wayward thoughts about teaching Miss Yelverton to ride and having *his* greedy hands about her supple waist instead of the groom's. He rode across his late cousin's acres towards his own Home Farm and tried hard to force his attention on to the hay harvest and crop rotations for next year. Anything to divert him from Miss Yelverton and a picture in his head of the shining curls she hid so carefully being fully revealed and perhaps even loose around her naked shoulders as she gazed adoringly into his eyes and… And damnation take it, here he was, mooning over the confounded woman in ways he ought to be thoroughly ashamed of yet again.

Now, where was he before a fantasy woman interrupted? Patting himself on the back for thinking about other things, if he recalled rightly—that should teach him never to be smug about Miss Yelverton again and avoid her instead of forcing her to join Aunt Tam and the children next time they visited Chantry Old Hall. At least the chances of Lucy being good for a whole week looked slim to impossible, so he should be spared at least one test of his resolve to forget the woman as anything other than what she wanted to be—confined to the schoolroom and unavailable in every sense of the word.

Then he thought about her days as an unwilling mantrap and shuddered on her behalf. If she was less determined and less canny at avoiding her mother's scheming, she might have wed a middle-aged icicle like his father. His mother must have sold herself for his father's riches and title, then hated the reality of life with him. A grand home and generous allowance could not have been enough to compensate for her loss of freedom, and trust his father to make sure there was precious little of that under his roof.

Harry could not recall even a hint of affection between them, although he was only five when his mother left. His strongest memory of her was the knot of tension in his belly when his father returned from some errand or duty he could not avoid and barked questions at her about who she had seen and what she had done with them while he was away. Then one morning his mother was gone. Her rooms still had the scent of roses and the light, feminine touches that always made them seem fascinating compared to the stiffness in the rest of the old house, but her absence felt brutal.

It was the servants who whispered to Harry that his mother had gone for good and was never coming back, so he had best stop driving his father into a fury with his questions about her. After a few cold silences, then a beating or two, Harry learned to do as he had been told and accept life as it was. Going to school had been a shock even so, especially when the school bullies delighted in telling him his mother was being kept by a rich and powerful lord while his father swore vengeance from afar and the *ton* laughed behind his back. Home for the summer, Harry had challenged his father with that tale and Sir Alfred had beaten him senseless for his trouble.

That was when Christian and his mother found

out and insisted Harry spend his vacations at Garrard House from then on. It was one beating he was almost grateful for, and from then on the bitter old man lived alone at Chantry Old Hall like a sulphurous dragon guarding his hoard and belching fire at anyone who tried to prise him away from it.

Harry's mother died while he was at Oxford and he supposed he ought to have felt something, but she knew what Harry's life would be like when she left and did it anyway, so he decided not to bother. The lesson of his parents' marriage was not to marry if you did not have to and, luckily, he did not have to. Bram would inherit Chantry Old Hall and Harry could forget his secret fantasy of a governess being all a man wanted in a woman if only she would let herself. She would never let herself, so that was that.

It seemed such a shame Garrard House was only a mile from Sir Harry's ancestral home as the crow flew. Even by the roundabout road that wound around the edge of one valley, then on to the next, it was only two miles to where Chantry Old Hall nestled above the wide Severn Plain with a view all the way to Wales on a clear day. A greater distance might have deterred him from visiting the children so often. For a year and a half Viola had been waiting for him to leave for the London Season, then the Little Season later in the year and after that for hunting weekends, then Christmas house parties with his fast friends.

Instead he stayed on at Chantry Old Hall as if he was an ordinary country gentleman, so deeply in love with his lavish acres and ancient house he hated to leave it. He had let the fun and frivolity of two London spring Seasons pass him by now, but surely he would be off to hunt over flatter ground for the autumn this year, then go on to join his friends for the Little Season. He had mourned his cousin and Mrs Marbeck as solemnly as anyone could expect— a lot more solemnly than most would have done, if the truth be told. He had done everything he could to make sure his wards were cared for and as happy as they could be under such circumstances. So why was the annoying man still here?

A good many of his fashionable, pleasure-loving friends had come to stay with him, of course, but Viola wished they would drag him off to Brighton for the summer so she could forget all about this silly temptation to ride across the park to join their larks and misdeeds and do the scandalous things the local gossips loved to cluck and exclaim over whenever they thought she was not listening.

It was only the allure of the unattainable that made him so unforgettable, she assured herself. Sir Harry Marbeck would not look at her twice if she was served up to him naked on a platter instead of his dinner one fine night. *Or maybe he would and then...* Wicked Viola whispered all sorts of exotic fantasies the rest of her was deeply shocked she even knew about. The sensible governess in her was delighted he had absently bowed in her direction before he left today, as if already forgetting the children's governess and Lucy's sulks in his haste to get back to the real business of life.

Yet Viola still wondered if Sir Harry had his own hard memories of the wrench away from home and security into the rough and tumble of school to stop him leaving the children here with her and letting them sink or swim without him. Maybe he had been bullied, although, as she thought of the tall and powerful man he was now, that idea seemed ridiculous. Still, she felt an ache in her gut at the thought of masters or older boys being cruel to the sensitive young boy she was suddenly convinced he had been.

A silly part of her longed to gently coax the story she sensed behind his brilliant façade of a devil-may-care rake out, then calm him with soothing and maybe even loving words, until he knew he could confide anything in her and she would not flinch away, or think him a fool for hanging on to memories that were best forgotten.

Stupid, stupid female, she raged at herself now she sat in front of her interrupted letter to her sister and tried to put Sir Harry Marbeck out of her head. She definitely would not go over to the window and watch him ride away from Garrard House. She stared at the abandoned letter and told herself she was only going to look at the garden and think about what to say next. He had interrupted her and made her lose her thread completely, and letters needed thinking out, since they cost so much to receive and Darius could not afford to pay for more sheets than necessary.

She stood at the window and strained her eyes for

even a glimpse of a fine and vigorous gentleman on his fine and vigorous horse, and maybe she was too late. Ah, no, there he was. He had taken his superbly cut coat off in the heat of the day and disposed of the light waistcoat that must have been nigh on roasting him as well. Viola held her breath as she built a picture of him in her head because she was too far away to truly see.

His snowy white shirt would be plastered against his muscular torso by the speed of his going. The easy strength in his thighs and the energy of him as he rode like the wind was as plain to her as if she was up there on the hillside with him and had an intimate view of his every move, hatless and heedless of sun and wind. The speed of his passing must spin out of still air, as even from here she could see that he rode like a centaur. He would be able to feel the might and muscle of a fine horse moving in perfect harmony with his rider under him and glory in it as a constrained lady like herself never could.

She closed her eyes and imagined herself riding by his side as the daredevil tomboy she had once been instead. Maybe she could even be plastered against his back as fondly as his discarded coat as they rode pillion and laughed into the wind, gloried in their speed and youth and all the things they were together. Her hands could explore that powerful body of his— her arms wrapped shamelessly around his narrow waist as he moved lithe and strong with the powerful horse, his wild spirit encouraging her to let all her inhibitions go and be wild and exhilarated and so alive it would feel almost immortal for one end-less, precious, glorious moment of pure joy as they rode on without a care in the world.

As fantasies went, it was a wistful, hurtful impos-sibility she had best forget as soon as she conjured it out of nothing. She turned away from the memory of that quick flash of Harry far off and coatless as he rode away from her as if she did not matter, because she did not. Not to him anyway. So she glared down into the garden as she had promised herself she was going to do when she came to stand here.

A pair of turtle doves sat on the sundial in the rose garden, cooing and bobbing simple love at one another. They seemed so oblivious to the world and its dangers and pitfalls. Life looked simple for turtle doves and maybe it was. They saw a mate, fell in love and got on with billing and cooing about it until there were lots of little turtle doves to feed and be busy with. Perhaps they fell out of love then, but she re-minded herself they had raised their family already, so maybe not. Maybe some love endured for turtle doves and even for one or two very lucky people.

She could hardly claim her big sister Marianne's love had not endured—her beloved Daniel's death in battle had left Marianne so starkly alone with her memories and a deep and abiding grief so power-ful it had physically hurt Viola to watch her suffer such loneliness and hopelessness that she was be-yond human comfort.

Ah, so there it was, then—her lesson in why it was folly to tumble into a love so deep you could never climb out of it. After all those years on the marriage mart, wondering why she could not feel even a pinch of love or desire for a single one of her would-be suitors, she realised it was because love became a pit in which to trap you when you lost the love you had so rashly risked everything for. That was what her big sister's doomed love affair had taught her and it was the perfect reminder why Viola had resolved never to fall into it at the tender age of sixteen. At least she had not told Harry about that when she let out so much about her silly, soiled past.

Seven years on, she still recalled the door of their shared bedchamber closing so softly behind her sister the night Marianne left home to find that love. Nobody else in the sleeping house had heard a thing or sensed anything was wrong, but Viola had known; she'd held her breath even when Marianne was beyond her sight and sharpened senses.

She felt for any creaks or protests from the noisy stair halfway down just as her sister must have done as she stole out into the night to catch the stage at the local inn to find her precious Daniel and make it impossible for him to do aught but marry her, despite all his scruples and refusal to let her take such a tumble in rank from clergyman's daughter to common soldier's wife. Except his was the only life Marianne wanted to share, and they managed to live strongly and happily for five years together before disaster struck.

But that happiness only made it worse when Marianne came home truly heartbroken over her Daniel, killed at the Battle of Badajoz. Nothing Viola could say or do could pierce the misery that wrapped her big sister like a shroud when she came back from Spain to endure a dull and respectable life in Bath as an ordinary soldier's widow under their parents' cramped roof.

The uncomfortable truth was Viola could not live with her sister's grief and leapt at this chance to leave Bath. She told herself the needs of three bereft children were greater than a grown woman who would not, or could not, talk to her sister. Marianne should have known better than to fall in love with a serving soldier and expect a long and settled life to grow out of their mutual obsession and defiance of the conventions.

Viola had to brush aside the familiar guilt of taking this post to avoid her sister's misery for more than a snatched visit last year, when Sir Harry had insisted on those two weeks he had promised her to visit her family. She deserved to struggle with this stupid infatuation with an impossible and unsuitable man for running away from Marianne when she needed her more than ever before. That night all those years ago, when she had heard the door close behind her sister, Viola had felt so alone as she lay and sobbed silently into her pillow, guiltily praying someone would wake up and catch Marianne before she could get clean away.

Instead she left Viola to face the hysterics and wild reproaches when Mama found out what Marianne had done. Yet, even knowing all that was to come, Viola did not wake the household and make sure her sister could not leave to wed a mere soldier under her own brother's command. And so the day had come when they received the letter to say the deed was done and Miss Marianne Yelverton was Mrs Daniel Turner.

With Marianne's sad example in front of her, how could she be such a fool? Viola wondered gloomily. She absently stared down at those billing and cooing doves while she tried to get that impossible picture of herself and Harry riding together all love-locked and besotted out of her head. Differences of rank were not swallowed up by love—Marianne and Daniel's story was an example of what went wrong if you tried. There was no chance Sir Harry Marbeck would fall in love with a governess. If she was not far more careful, she would reveal her feelings for him.

She had to make sure this feral, foolish attraction never got as far as she imagined it might just now. Becoming the lover of a man who could not love her back would be the ultimate disaster and kill her secret dream of opening a school of her own one day with a scandal so wide she would be lucky to end up as a housemaid in a respectable house. No, the very idea of it was simply not to be contemplated, so it was about time she stopped doing it.

Chapter Six

'Why won't they go faster?' Lucy asked as the team pulling the stately barouche Sir Harry had sent down for his aunt and wards made a long, slow progress up the hill to Chantry Old Hall on a hot day.

'Because they have to make the extra effort of pulling you up the hill for a treat I still do not think you deserve, young lady,' Miss Marbeck informed her with a frown. 'I would keep quiet and be grateful in your shoes.'

'Look at that fawn, Lucy,' Emma said and distracted Lucy and her great-aunt to avoid yet another argument.

'If I had a bow, I could shoot it from here,' Bram put in simply to annoy everyone, as far as Viola could see, and even she began to wonder if she might have a headache before the afternoon was over.

'That you could not,' his great-aunt snapped with a harried glance at Viola as if to say this was her job, so why was she having to do it for her?

Probably because the lady would be very annoyed if the governess stepped in and took her authority away. Knowing she could not do right for being wrong when Miss Marbeck was too hot and missing her old, quiet life, Viola bit back a sigh and tried to look innocent and oblivious at the same time.

'This is the wrong time of year, even if Uncle Harry allowed horrid little boys to shoot at his deer, which he never will,' Emma said with a glower for her little brother that said even she was tired of him today.

'And nobody should shoot at fawns,' Lucy said, tears standing in her eyes as if she believed her big brother's bravado even if nobody else did.

'Quite right, Lucy.' Viola spoke up to stop a flood of tears spoiling their entrance and what promised to be a wonderful day for the children, if not for their elders who must chase after them in this heat to keep them out of trouble. 'Bram would not dream of doing so even if he had a bow, which fortunately he does not, would you, Bramford?'

'No, Miss Yelverton,' Bram agreed with a sigh at the use of his full name. He considered it ridiculous for a warrior in waiting, and she only used it to let him know he had reached his limits and had better stop.

'Why did you say you would, then?' Lucy demanded sulkily and still looked tearful. Viola took a closer look at her youngest pupil and wondered if her high colour was entirely caused by the heat and too much excitement, but of course they were reason enough.

'You know perfectly well your brother delights in being contrary, just like his little sister,' Miss Marbeck snapped. 'Now be quiet, all of you. I have the headache,' the lady added with a frown.

'Should we stop and have the grooms put the hood up to keep the sun out of your eyes, ma'am?' Viola asked, smothering a craven wish she had found a good enough excuse to avoid this hot and tedious drive. Then there were the next few hours doing her best to pretend the master of Chantry Old Hall was nothing out of the common way to look forward to. She wished he had not got that almost promise to come on the family's next visit to his home out of her last week.

'Ridiculous, anyone would think I was in my dotage,' Miss Marbeck said contrarily.

'Not for long,' Viola muttered.

'I heard that,' the lady said sharply and shot Viola an impatient glare. 'You are almost as much trouble as three restless, quarrelsome children this afternoon, Madam. At least they have the excuse of being too young to know better.'

'It isn't an excuse. You said so,' Bram said sulkily, and for once Viola could only agree with him. His Great-Aunt Tam was in one of those moods where nothing anyone could do or say would be right, so they might as well stop trying.

'Better than what?' Lucy added.

If Viola knew that, she would not be sitting here,

dreading her next sight of Sir Harry Marbeck, hero of all her most foolish dreams. What a pity he did not go back to town and take up his old louche and reckless life again, she decided gloomily. Her inner houri argued that might break her silly heart, but if that was so, it would break in six and a bit months' time anyway. She could leave Garrard House then and how she would miss these contrary, bright, beloved children. But pretending she felt nothing for Sir Harry was slowly driving her demented, and frustrated, and out of temper with him and most of the rest of the world. And the children and Miss Marbeck did not deserve to endure her nerves being constantly on edge and her temper with it because of this silly obsession with the wretched man.

'Better than I do today.' Miss Marbeck answered Lucy's impossible question.

No doubting the lady would need some peace and quiet before she was ready to set off back down this hill again, whether she had a headache or not. That would mean Viola staying with the children and their beloved Uncle Harry while his aunt was soothed and quieted into a better frame of mind to face the journey back down the hill to Garrard House.

Botheration! Miss Yelverton wanted to shout. *Ooh, how lovely, a whole afternoon of delicious temptation to revel in*, crooned the other Viola, and she squirmed in her seat like an overexcited debutante, reckless little fool that she was.

At least their great-aunt's irritable reply had silenced the children, and even Lucy had stopped fidgeting when the carriage finally reached the fine plateau at the top of the twisting and turning drive designed to make the slope gentler for horses. Now they were bowling along a fine avenue of oak trees and the shade felt such a relief after the heat of a relentless late summer sun. There was nothing much to see until the trees thinned and a fine vista of the ancient and golden stone house opened out from this grand entrance to the grounds. Even when you knew about it, that view still made the breath catch in your lungs at the grandeur and beauty of the place, Viola decided wistfully.

Today the late summer sun was reflected from sparkling leaded windows and the golden light seemed to have seeped into the very stones of the place, as if storing warmth up against the coming chill of winter. That season seemed very far away in this sulky heat as they emerged from the mighty trees. *Only one more winter and the early spring for you to get through now, though,* Viola reminded herself as Sir Harry came running down the impressive flight of steps some long-dead Marbeck had added to make his consequence even more obvious to visitors. To distract herself from the compelling sight of his youth and power and golden good looks, Viola decided the later front and elaborate portico of his house must have been added to the medieval core of the house. It looked newer than the Tudor courtyards and long gallery that should have made it a piecemeal jumble but somehow did not.

The size and rambling stateliness of his grand

mansion should put a brake on her silly dreams. She was an unsuitable young woman; he was a rich and well-connected baronet. And he was waiting at the bottom of all those stately steps to bid his family welcome and she was not part of it. Viola sighed and decided nobody could accuse him of being toplofty, though it might be better for her if she could.

'Good afternoon,' Sir Harry greeted them cheerfully, and what did he know? It was not a good afternoon; it was a hot and sticky and potentially disastrous afternoon where nothing felt quite as it ought to. If she could feel the threat of thunder in the air and feel fretful tempers about to break into open rebellion, he ought to sense the tension in their hot and shiny faces as well.

'Uncle Harry!' Lucy cried with an open delight.

Viola told herself off for the envy she felt as the little girl tumbled out of the carriage the moment the horses came to a halt. Indeed, it only took her that long because Viola had grabbed the strings of her pinafore to make sure she could not leap out sooner and take a tumble. 'I missed you,' Lucy added as she dashed headlong at him, holding up her arms to be picked up.

He obliged with a wry smile. 'It must be nearly a whole week since we saw one another last, Little Miss Impatience,' he said ruefully, but hitched the little girl up on one arm so he could lean over and hug Emma with his other since she was too old and dignified to scramble all over him as well. 'A very good day to you, young man,' he said as he held out his hand to be shaken solemnly, since Bram considered himself far too old and manly to be hugged, except when he had a nightmare or nobody else was looking.

'Aunt Tam,' the man added with a charming grin to excuse leaving his aunt and the most senior member of the party until nearly last as he leaned forward to kiss her on the cheek with Lucy still clinging to him like a limpet on a rock. 'And how are you today, my darling?'

'Ha!' his darling aunt barked, as if she was not in the least bit flattered, but of course she was. 'Much you care. Stopping away all week, then making us labour up that hill in this heat just to get a sight of you, you rogue. And I suppose you must have been entertaining those fast friends of yours all week, and their shenanigans kept you away from Garrard House. Well, I hope they have all gone now, since I have no desire to get back in that bone-shaking carriage of yours until I have had a rest, and I will have to if any of the fools you like to mix with are still here.'

'I have not been entertaining fools of any sort, Auntie dearest. I was away from home for a day or two. I had business in Oxford,' her nephew replied with a thoughtful look at her hot and weary face and a fleeting frown that agreed with Viola's assessment that the lady was not pretending to be tired and out of sorts this time. 'Therefore the only fool you need to avoid today is me,' he said lightly because no doubt he knew even better than Viola did that sympathy with her headache or her rheumatism or whatever was ailing her would not please his aunt one bit.

'You never spoke a truer word, you young flibbertigibbet. You really are a fool if you want to live in this great barn of a place all on your own except for those fly-by-night friends of yours. When are you going to get married and take life seriously for once?'

'Hmm, now let me think,' he said, pretending to consider the idea. 'Ah, yes, that will be never,' he answered so easily Viola had to put another piece of her heart into an imaginary ice house and lock the door. She knew he would never wed the likes of her, even if he was eagerly hanging out for a wife—which he most definitely was not—so she could not imagine why it hurt so much to have to put even more of her true self in the dark and the cold like that. He would never see her as a relatively young and almost attractive lady after her disastrous confession of her past life as a husband hunter.

He will never want you back with this stupid, relentless need that keeps making up impossible dreams of him as your besotted lover, whatever you confess to him, Viola Yelverton, the governess scolded her inner idiot.

'And a very good day to you, Miss Yelverton,' the man said politely, almost as if she was an afterthought.

'Good day, Sir Harry,' she replied woodenly.

'I apologise for the heat, my wards' fidgets and the fact my aunt must have been carping about them all the way up here, to make matters even worse,' he added, as if he could read the fatigue on her averted face and was moved to pity her when she did not want him to.

'I doubt you arranged for any of it to happen,' she said shortly.

'No, I have no power over the elements, my aunt or these three scallywags,' he said with a wry grimace at his wards. 'Knowing you three cannot survive more than half an hour without food, I persuaded Cook to lay out enough of it to feed a small army in the Garden Room. There will be no fighting over who has what and how much of it, mind, and if I hear you have been stealing from your sisters' plates again, there will be no cake for you for a whole week, young man,' he warned Bram before all three children ran around the side of the house and through a side door they knew would be open for them, whooping with delight as they went and sounding as if they had not been fed for days.

'I had better go with them,' Viola hastily excused herself, but walked into Sir Harry's outstretched arm. She stopped as if she had hit a solid wall, and the sudden contact with his heavily muscled forearm seemed to reach into every fibre of her body. Goodness, he did a lot of riding and whatever else he did to keep fit as an athlete.

'No, please stay,' he said as he absently rubbed his arm, as if he had been scorched by their closeness, too. 'Their nanny and nursery maid have had time to rest after their journey up here in advance. Cook has half her staff waiting to cluck over the children as well and is looking forward to the melee for some reason. Best if you stay out of the way and enjoy some peace and quiet while you can,' he added smoothly enough.

'Thank you,' she said, deciding the idea would be wonderful if she wasn't already flustered by his very masculine presence on such a hot and sticky afternoon. Peace *was* a rare commodity with the children so full of energy, and a cup of tea sounded wonderful after her hectic morning battling the children's excitement over treats to come. At least Lucy had wanted this so badly that she had been good for nearly a week and, yes, perhaps she did deserve to escape Viola and Miss Marbeck's scrutiny to make an even better reward for such a mighty effort.

Harry escorted the ladies up the steps and felt his aunt lean on his arm as if she really needed his support. He still found time to tingle with awareness of Miss Yelverton even as she tried to lag behind them. He wondered if the stubborn woman might disappear if he turned his back for too long, since she was being even quieter and more mouse-like today. He listened for her soft footfall on stone as they made their way into the house and felt almost like an anxious lover. At least the heat had stopped her wearing boots so she could tramp the hills with his wards instead of spending any time with him. Until today, he had thought any gown would be an improvement on the grey monstrosity she usually wore, but the mudgrey poplin she was wearing proved him wrong. She must feel close to fainting under the ridiculous cap she wore to snuff out any remaining youth and beauty the world might catch a glimpse of.

No rustle of slinky silk petticoats or gauzy underskirts for Miss Yelverton, of course. If Glory was here to brazenly climb the front steps at his side, she would be languid, with the whisper of her skirts meant to fascinate and seduce her keeper, but his former mistress was in Brighton now, so best forget how different the underpinnings of courtesan and governess would be. Plain cotton or linen would still be seductive with a Miss Yelverton under them. *Curse it—down, boy*, he silently ordered his unruly manhood and tried to pretend he was listening to his aunt's list of reasons why today's trip up the hill was a terrible idea and where had he been all week?

He could shock Miss Yelverton and his aunt by admitting he was in Oxford to see his ex-mistress off in comfort. But Aunt Tam would be delighted Glory was gone. Despite him pointing out he did not need an heir whenever she gave him a chance, she would tell him he was a fool, then push the belles of the Cotswolds at him to show him what he was missing. Not that he was missing them, just a stubbornly aloof governess who was seductive and dangerous without trying.

'Just now I prefer your room to your company, Nephew,' Aunt Tam told him abruptly once they were inside the airy entrance hall, but he ushered her into the grand Saloon she always complained was draughty as a barn and settled her in a well-padded

chair before he took her at her word, since he could
tell nothing he did would be right until she slept off
her megrims.

'And you can go away as well, young woman,'
Aunt Tam added irritably to confirm the wisdom of
that idea. 'I can't abide fussing and I refuse to snore
in public,' she added, as if that explained everything,
and perhaps it did.

'I would not tell anyone,' Miss Yelverton said in-
dignantly, as if she wanted to stay here and avoid
him, and that hurt.

Apparently she could not imagine anything worse
on a hot afternoon than a stroll through his gardens
in his company. He was just a fool who tortured himself with fantasies of her suddenly becoming recep-
tive to his sensual attention and deliciously cool and
sweet as ice cream on a hot day. If only she wanted
him back, they could get into all sorts of sensual
mischief behind Aunt Tam's back. Oh, damnation,
now he must leave Miss Yelverton somewhere suitable while he conjured up glaciers and ice houses
and the killing frosts of a deep midwinter. After half
an hour or so of that, maybe his sex could forget his
heady fantasy of heating up Miss Yelverton in the
most delightful fashion and never mind the weather.

'Would you care to look through the pile of books
I brought back from Oxford while my aunt is busy
thinking with her eyes closed, Miss Yelverton? That
way you can see if there is anything useful for the
children without them clamouring to see it first. I
shall go and find out what they are up to so you have

time to examine them in peace,' he said, flattering himself he almost sounded as distantly polite to her as she usually was to him. Hmm, did that mean she always had to hide an edgy awareness of him as he must go on fighting his fantasy of her carried away by passion in his arms? *Highly unlikely, Marbeck,* he told himself scornfully as he hurried towards the less formal wing of the house before she could argue it was her duty to accompany him.

Chapter Seven

'Aye, do as my nephew says, my girl; somebody ought to,' Miss Marbeck urged Viola as the sound of his hasty footsteps faded on the fine marble floors of his fine house. She waved Viola out of the room with an ironic smile that could say a lot if Viola chose to notice.

At least the library was on the morning side of the house and cool as anywhere could be on a day like today, as the butler helpfully pointed out while she was standing in the hall feeling a bit lost and very unwanted.

'Thank you,' Viola said as she strolled towards the library, trying to pretend it had not hurt her when Sir Harry had sped off as if he could not wait to get away from her. Until today, she thought she and Miss Marbeck enjoyed a guarded sort of friendship as well. Apparently she was wrong and Miss Marbeck preferred her room to her company, as did her nephew. Oh, well, she only had six months left on her promise now and maybe Miss Marbeck would be as relieved to get back to her old peaceful life as Viola would be to return to Miss Thibett's school.

If the girls went with her, of course, and Bram went to the wonderful prep school she was beginning to dread Sir Harry finding for him, they could all leave Garrard House at the same time. She would miss any of the Marbeck children she was separated from quite dreadfully, and the thought of them living here with a new governess, who might not love them as much as she did, made her heart ache.

The neatly regimented life of a good school she had once yearned for as a refuge seemed dull as ditch water now, and there was just no pleasing some people, was there? She told herself not to be a fool and grasp the promise of leaving in six months' time like a drowning man at a lifeline. She leafed through a fine atlas and a fascinating book on exotic animals she knew Lucy would love, if only for its finely tinted and expensive engravings. There was an amusing book of fables for Emma and an adventurous-looking collection of tales for Bram. It was because she was so hot and tired her eyes watered at the care Sir Harry had taken over choosing exactly the right book for each child. Or did he pay someone to select books for his wards instead? No, that was unjust. For a fanciful moment Viola let herself dream his rackety reputation was a smokescreen to hide his scholarly nature.

Then she let the memory of him grinning at his aunt like the cock of the walk and handsome as pure sin back in and knew he'd earned his raffish reputation fairly and squarely. Right, then, back to the books. She was not in the least bit jealous he could show his lovely mistress the full range of his passions and transgressions, share ardent and urgent kisses with her and consign the governess to a pile of admittedly fine books as if that was her birthright, just as his lovely mistress was born to command masculine attention wherever she went. Harry might even let *That Woman*, as his aunt called her, see the real man under all his clever disguises, but Miss Viola Yelverton could only be interested in books and not men like Sir Harry Marbeck. Today she could not help resenting the difference, even though she certainly did not want to be his mistress.

Better to be Miss Yelverton, with a lifetime of rewarding work ahead and the satisfaction of doing it well. *Oh, yes, what a very good thing that you are you and not his mistress, Viola,* she told herself. She snapped the last of the books closed and added it to the pile to be sent down to Garrard House for the children. They would distract them from disappointment at the end of their splendid afternoon. And at the end of her six months she would return to Bath and teach hopeful young ladies once again and be glad of it. Maybe one day she could retire to a cottage on Darius's estate and be a proper aunt and great-aunt to his children and grandchildren.

That reminded her—she must ask Sir Harry's permission to attend her brother's hasty wedding. She managed a grin at the memory of Darius's letter, demanding she get there by hook or by crook, and concluded he was fathoms deep in love with his Fliss. Viola suddenly longed for him and for her sister. Marianne was her confidant as a girl and she would listen to her little sister's troubles without judgement now. She might even soothe and comfort her as she had when they were girls. Then perhaps she would come up with a few practical solutions or sage advice. A pity they were fifty miles apart and it was Viola's fault it felt like a bigger gulf than simple distance could explain.

'Well, do you think they will do?' Sir Harry's voice interrupted her reverie from the doorway and made her jump, then her heart race at his sudden presence without any warning from her senses he was coming.

'Yes, they are perfect. You chose well,' she told him with a genuine smile because she could not help being pleased to see him despite this ridiculous feeling of breathlessness and the wicked tingle at the heart of her she had been fighting since the first day she set eyes on him.

'High praise indeed,' he said, looking a little bit startled by the unusual warmth of her welcome.

'I do give it where it is due,' she said defensively. 'Although I must be a very poor teacher if my employer finds that so hard to believe.'

'No, I don't; I have often heard you be soft-hearted and kind to my brats, and you tolerate my aunt's irritable moods and eccentricities with patience and good humour. Since you save your best disapproving looks for me, I have to suppose I must deserve them.'

'They are not solely for you,' she argued reck-lessly. 'I sometimes use one on Lucy and Bram as well.'

'Aye, you need to, although Emma is far too hard on herself for either of us to need any for her.'

'She is indeed; I still worry about her.'

'So do I. You are very good at turning a subject, Miss Yelverton. It is one trick of yours I would be sorry to see Lucy copying.'

'She has plenty of tricks of her own without learn-ing any from me,' Viola said and shot him a frown because she felt dangerously undefended now his blue eyes were resting thoughtfully on her, as if he was seeing her as a woman for the first time. Her breath caught in her lungs and she made herself breathe out a long, slow breath to calm the racing of her stupid heart. He would notice she was trying to control agitation and not fury if she was not very careful. Then he might think harder about what made her tick as a woman rather than a governess and come up with one or two uncomfortable answers. She did not think she could endure the embarrassment when he watched her with pity, then walked away.

'Maybe you are right,' he said softly. Now there was open speculation as well as surprise in his eyes when she looked up from the books again and he was still there. In fact, he was closer than he was before, and she was quite sure he had been on his way to keep watch over his aunt when impulse made him stop and ask her a question about these books instead. Ah, yes, books—that was why they were both in here, was it not?

'Much as we all love her, I know Lucy is a minx in the making, Sir Harry,' Viola said in order to push his attention back on to his youngest ward and not her governess.

'As long as we can teach her to have a conscience about her mischief and manipulative habits, I would not have her change into a pattern card of all the virtues for all the tea in China. Lucy has character,' he said, allowing himself to be led away from more dangerous subjects, even if part of his mind looked as if it was still busy with Viola's foibles and not his youngest ward's, judging by the preoccupied frown between his brows and the speculative look in his eyes.

'Yes, she has enough of that to supply half a dozen small girls with more of it than is good for them. However, we women must still live within the narrow limits set for us by our society, Sir Harry, and it can be very hard for a girl like her to realise how narrow they truly are,' she added, her own shock at the discovery of how little her life was going to be after Marianne left home sore in her memory. 'You will do Lucy no favours if you raise her to expect better of the world than it is willing to give,' she warned him quite seriously.

'Were you as full of character and mischief once upon a time as well, then, Miss Yelverton? You have learned that lesson a little too well, if so. I would not want Lucy slamming against the unfair divisions of this bad old world as hard as you must have done.'

He had as good as called her a disappointed and repressed woman and, for heaven's sake, he was right, wasn't he? 'Lucy will grow up in more favourable circumstances,' she argued. 'And I suppose her character and your high expectations for her could help her make good choices one day,' she added more warily.

'With my expectations of the man she may one day want to marry to back them up, I can safely promise you Lucy will have all the advantages I can give her. And the idiot had best watch his step if he dares to even think about disappointing her while I am above ground.'

Viola did not doubt it. He would be a strong and cynical protector for a pair of sheltered young girls whenever Emma and Lucy needed one. Wanting him as a defensive wall between her and the rest of the world, as well as for his own handsome and compelling sake, was ridiculous of her, though. 'It will be a long time before any of us need to worry about him, and where is Lucy at the moment, by the way?'

'The children's old nanny and the nursery maid took them to run off their excesses in the maze. I doubt they can get up to much mischief in there and they can get happily lost while their luncheon goes down.'

'Oh, good,' she said half-heartedly because that was an excuse to go after them she no longer had.

'And Aunt Tam is fast asleep,' he added to make

them being alone inside and wide awake feel even more dangerous.

'I doubt she has slept much lately in this heat.'

'I dare say not,' he said. 'It has been very sultry.'

'Yes, very,' she replied, and it felt like a waste for him to be lying sleepless a mile away from her hot and airless bedchamber. It was flattering and just a little bit too exciting, to look up and see a speculative look in his eyes, as if he was not quite sure he had her measure after all. Maybe she should not have told him about her miserable adventures in her small and local society, so unlike his dashing circle of friends, but it had made him see her as more than a prim and proper schoolmistress. After a year and a half of lonely yearning for more than an absent nod or word of greeting from him, that did feel rather wonderful.

'The children have been restless as well. Lucy was awake at some unearthly hour this morning and, of course, she had to go and wake the others as well,' she managed to say, despite a strong urge to simply stand here and simper up at him.

'You must sometimes long for a little peace and quiet,' he said, as if he wanted to know more about her life for once rather than rushing off to do something more important.

'Now and again, perhaps, but they are lively and interesting children.'

'A little too much so at times,' he said ruefully, and she laughed.

'Of course, but think how bored we would be

if they suddenly turned into good little storybook angels.'

'Sometimes it's good to dream,' he said with such rueful warmth she smiled at him like an idiot.

'Sometimes,' she echoed.

'Like now,' he murmured, and how had he come so close without them both noticing and politely backing away from one another as they usually did?

'Indeed,' she agreed.

'I dream about you,' he admitted huskily.

Now it was too late to take that step back and then another somehow. She stood and waited for him to decide whether he was going to come any closer as they both seemed to want him to deep down. And here he was.

'It makes it devilish hard to sleep during all these hot and humid nights we have been having lately, Miss Yelverton,' he murmured.

'Me, too,' she said, and as he bent his head even closer to catch her words, she whispered the next ones even as his warmth and masculine scent and sheer closeness made her knees wobble. 'I feel so restless sometimes.'

'Indeed?' he replied huskily, and then he did the unthinkable—he kissed her, and she made it easy for him by tilting her head up at exactly the right angle to meet his mouth, as if that was what they were both here for.

It was gentle and playful and she even felt the curve of his mouth as he smiled into hers and savoured it, tasting her with a delicate touch of his exploring lips and tongue, as if he had to sip first in order not to scare her off. *As if I am so easily scared*, she silently chided and smiled back against his deliciously firm mouth and opened her suddenly very heavy-lidded eyes to shoot him a witchy and inviting look from under her lashes. It worked; oh, yes, it definitely did that.

She felt her legs wobble and her senses reel as he took her challenge and doubled it. Heat such as she had never even dared to dream of shot through her as his lips urged hers open and he plunged his tongue into her mouth and danced with hers the second she yielded. She curved her body into his so their contact could shiver right through her and felt as if everything he was kissed all she was for an emphatic, electric moment.

It was like warm lightning, like enchantment and unthinkable, sweetest heat all rolled into one. She heard herself murmur something wordless yet emphatic and tried to beat away the memory that grand Chantry Old Hall was all around them and his aunt and the children and all those servants were far too close by for this to be as right as it felt. He seemed to wake up to them all out there as well at the soft sound of her gasp of need and wanting. She felt regret in his mouth as he firmed it on hers for one last, lingering intimacy of a kiss, then raised his head so she could feel his quickened breath on her lips. And feel the fact of his hands on her body, his fingers splayed on her backside where he had shaped her shamelessly

closer to his mighty body, so they were wound together like the almost lovers they so nearly were.

She could think about that later and wonder why
no memory of her revulsion when other men tried to
force such intimacy on her stepped in to sicken her
about what they were doing and the depths it could
lead them into if they were not very careful. This was
nothing like the terror and revulsion those other men
inflicted on her in the hope of forcing what she would
not give up willingly. He was nothing like them. He
was Harry and only himself, and that might have
been enough for both of them if she was different.

'I apologise,' he said huskily and looked horribly guilty.

'Please, do not,' she said, stepping back from him
and shaking her head because words were less than
actions as she tried to bring her logical mind back
down to earth and get them both out of this mess
without further damage. 'I really do not want you
to,' she added, and at least she knew what she meant.

He did not look as if he did as she pushed herself
further away, then stood on her own two feet and
even managed a few more steps to put the library
desk between her and him, not because she was suddenly revolted by what they had done but because she
was afraid she might reach for him again. He looked
a lot less willing for them to be so deliciously, inti-
mately close again than she was.

'I ought—' he began to say, but she held up an
imperious hand to cut him off before he could go on
with the sentence she could see coming.

'No, you ought not. I am not a mantrap nowadays, Sir Harry.'

'Of course not,' he argued with a lot more passion now he seemed to have got his proper senses back in working order. 'If a man had said that about you, I would call him out on the spot.'

'Lucky I am not a man, then,' she joked weakly and saw him frown fiercely, then begin to thaw as he caught her unexpected humour in this impossibly awkward situation. It felt far more tempting to stay here and learn the depths and widths of what they had in common than to hastily promise all intimacy between them was forgotten and best never even thought about again, by either of them, ever.

'Oh, you are definitely not one of those,' he told her with such hot appreciation in his eyes that they were almost back to that delicious, dangerous mutual fascination again when footsteps scurried in the hall and the butler's voice raised a protest.

Chapter Eight

'Miss Yelverton! Oh, miss, you must come quick,' Carrie the nursery maid shouted over the man's indignant reproach for running and being in the front of the house in the first place.

Viola heard panic in the maid's voice and never mind petty rules about who was supposed to be where. She ran out of the library, heart racing at the sound of so much fear in the girl's frantic plea. 'What is it? What happened?' she demanded as she met the maid in the hall.

'It's Master Bram. He's fallen,' the maid managed to gasp between hoarse breaths, and at any other time Viola would have ordered her to sit down and recover before she went further, but terror forbade it now.

'Where?' she demanded and wanted to shake the information out of the girl.

'The boathouse roof. Master Bram climbed up—'

'How the devil did he get up there?' Harry demanded.

Whatever else the girl was going to say was lost as Viola decided she had heard enough and ran down the steps like a greyhound after a hare. She would have blindly dashed on and been winded before she got the half a mile to the other side of the ornamental lake from this side of the house. What on earth was Bram doing on the roof of the boathouse when he was supposed to be playing safely in the maze with his sisters? Never mind that now. Bram and Lucy's genius for getting into trouble ought to have warned her not to take her eyes off them for even half a minute, and she was furious with herself for kissing Harry while they were roaming about the place without her now.

'No, not that way! We need a horse to get him back here as fast as we can. I had best send for the doctor as well,' Harry said abruptly.

'True,' Viola conceded and changed tack to run to the palatial stables where his horses enjoyed the best of everything equine, including a luxury of grooms to tend to their every need.

'Thunderer!' He overtook her with ease to bark that order at his head groom. 'No saddle, just a bridle. There's no time,' he ordered and seemed about to dash in and do it himself when the man waved him back.

'He'll be excited if he sees you and act up, Sir Harry. Let me go.'

'Aye, and you, Abel—have my curricle brought out and the greys harnessed fast as you can, then drive Miss Yelverton to the boathouse as soon as it is ready,' he said to another groom.

'No, bring me a fast horse. No need for a saddle for me either,' Viola argued and was furious at the glare of impatience the groom and Harry shot her. Her temper fired and it felt better to be furious than scared half to death for the boy she had come to love. 'I used to ride out with Sir Edward Hopkin's lads as a girl, so I can manage anything you have in your stables riding astride,' she snapped impatiently at Harry.

How did they think she could stand about waiting to see what Bram had done to himself as if it did not matter very much? She had spent almost every day of the last year and a half battling past Bram's fury and grief and finding the strong-willed, brave and restless boy hiding behind his occasional insolence. She stamped her foot impatiently and wished she had set off running and ignored Harry and her own common sense.

'Sir Ned would not let her near his racing nags unless that's true,' Sir Harry conceded and nodded permission at the still dubious Abel. 'Dulcimer,' he ordered, 'and a guinea if you get a saddle on her before Culworth gets Thunderer out here.'

'Why?' Viola demanded hotly, again because being angry at his male superiority and overprotectiveness was better than picturing terrible things when she had time to think.

'Because it must be years since you rode the gallops like a hoyden. I am amazed your parents permitted it, by the way.'

'They never knew. I pretended to be a boy and Sir Ned pretended to believe me, since I could ride his trickiest horses and was light enough not to slow them down.'

'You must have taken some crashing falls even so.'

'I bounced and never mind that now. Here are our horses and you are a guinea the poorer, Sir Harry.'

'Cheap at the price,' he said with misplaced humour as she impatiently kirtled her skirts about her waist on the run and he ogled her petticoats like a stage villain.

'Just ride,' she ordered him abruptly as she sped over to the mounting block so nobody had to toss her on to the dancing filly impatiently waiting for her rider to get in the saddle and get on with whatever they were about to do.

They hardly spared one another a glance after Harry watched Viola gather the reins expertly and keep eager Dulcimer to a walk until it was safe for them to get to the lake as fast as the two thoroughbreds could go. The speed and exhilaration of being in the saddle of a fine horse again and free to ride properly blocked some of her panic, but the closer they got to the lake, the more dreadful images of what they might find took over her thoughts.

She was relieved when they finally got close enough to see Bram sitting on the grass, even if he did look very sorry for himself and soaking wet. The closer they were, the less sturdy Bram looked, and she could see he was being propped up by Emma on one side and a young gardener on the other. From the look of it, the sturdy youth had gone into the water to drag Bram out, and thank heavens the lad was nearby or this might have been another Marbeck tragedy. She refused to even consider that right now, although it would probably haunt her nightmares for years to come.

Even as she and Harry slowed their mounts to ride along the narrower path around the lake, she saw Bram drop on to all fours and retch pathetically until fury drained right out of her and she was just afraid. If he had swallowed that much water before he was fished out of the lake, it could be dangerous for a boy of Bram's years. He might be too young to escape half drowning himself unscathed, especially in a slow-flowing lake full of weed and mud and goodness knew what else.

'Ride back and order a tub filled with warm water at the double. We need a bath and a bedchamber ready to receive the little scoundrel the moment we get there,' Harry ordered Viola, as if he was a general supervising a battle and she was the nearest foot soldier.

She badly wanted to argue she was needed here, but logic said he was right and she must do what was best for Bram. She turned the filly's head and dug her heels in to hurry away. It felt so wrong to be going away from Bram and his sisters, but she controlled Dulcimer's attempts at arguing with the idea easily enough and urged her across the parkland as fast as they could go without adding to the list of injured when there was no time to waste.

Tossing the reins to an open-mouthed onlooker, she dashed back into the house with Sir Harry's orders sharp on her tongue. She was still fighting the urge to turn and run outside to meet him and the children while she ruthlessly hustled the flustered maids around with a breathless string of orders. Then she ran on up the stairs herself before shouting back the demand for hot water and towels that she cursed herself for forgetting in her panic and told herself to calm down.

She rapped out more orders for someone to light a fire in the grate of the first room she raced into, even if it was the end of August. She stripped off the holland covers and made the bed up herself when the flustered girls ran in with the bed linen and did not move fast enough for her. What the housekeeper made of the governess taking over her household as if she had every right was not important with these images of Bram struggling to get all that water out of his young lungs playing over and over in her head and urging her to hurry. Somehow she had to make sure everything that could be done to get the house ready to care for him was done by the time he got here.

'The doctor?' she gasped out and realised she could not hope to calm all this panic rolling about in her belly until she was sure he was going to survive his latest misdeed. At last the housekeeper sped into the room and tucked in the corners of an immaculate linen sheet on the other side of the bed from Viola. Then she shook down pillows into pristine pillowcases and shot Viola a stern look to tell her the same things she was trying so hard to tell herself.

'We have sent four grooms to look for him, so they can find him in whatever direction he went if he is from home, Miss Yelverton. Be assured he will get here as fast as Culworth can drive him,' the lady said sternly.

'How will he know which of them has found the doctor?'

'They each have a hunting horn.'

Satisfied all that could be done was being done, Viola ran out to hurry the maids and any available footmen with those cans of hot water and a hip bath because, never mind how well the household was organising itself now the initial shock had worn off, she could not simply stand here and wait.

The bath had barely been set in place and was being filled by a parade of servants with buckets and all sorts of odd containers when they heard the noise of wheels on the gravel sweep below. Viola ran down the wide oak stairs, narrowly avoiding the procession coming up, and skidded to a halt at the top of the steps outside the front door. She put her hands up to her heart, which felt as if it was beating out of her chest with apprehension, and stared at the procession rushing towards the house.

Abel was driving his master's sporting curricle and the girls were crammed together on the perch meant for a diminutive tiger. Bram was half-sitting, half-lying in the passenger seat, with Harry riding alongside to hold him steady. She ran down the steps to hold the horses' heads the moment Abel halted them, so that Harry could lift Bram off the seat, then up into his arms without delay.

How silly of her to feel as if all would be well now Harry had the boy safe as he grasped Bram close and ran towards the house with hardly a pause in his long stride. He leapt up the steps two by two, then in through the front door and was soon out of sight. Viola made herself stay behind and help the terrified girls down from their perch. Their pale faces and wide, frightened eyes told her that memories of losing both their parents in the blink of an eye made them even more fearful for their brother.

'Come now, my love. Try to at least pretend to be strong and hopeful for Lucy's sake,' Viola whispered to Emma after she lifted Lucy down first and watched her run in her uncle's wake as fast as her legs would go.

Maybe it was wrong to add to Emma's heavy load of cares, but the thought of her younger sister's terror did seem like the snap of reality Emma needed to push aside her own fears and hope for a better outcome. She nodded and gasped out a thank you for the help to get down from the carriage that nearly broke Viola's heart for her quietly adult manners of a girl still a month away from her twelfth birthday. Then they were down on solid ground and both of them ran for the stairs in Harry and Lucy's wake. Emma held Viola's hand all the way up them and she spared a moment to wonder who was comforting whom.

In the time it took to get the girls down and climb upstairs, Harry had got Bram into the bedroom and whisked him out of his wet and clinging clothes and placed him into the waiting tub. The greyish tinge to the boy's skin was already giving way to a faint wash of pink in the warm water, but Viola was worried about the dullness of Bram's usually bright eyes. Harry glanced her way as they shared silent fears for the boy the girls had best not know about.

'Hot bricks and a warming pan and hurry.' Viola rapped out the order to the now truly flustered and shocked housekeeper and was relieved when her tone seemed to snap the woman out of her stunned inertia.

'Right away, ma'am,' the housekeeper said and bustled away as if she would rather deal with them than watch another Marbeck family tragedy.

Not if I have anything to do with it, Viola resolved, as if she could stand between this sorrowful family and the chance Bram's misadventure would end so badly. 'We need to rub some warmth back into him, Sir Harry,' she said and saw a bruise already forming under Bram's dark curls, which explained at least some of his lethargy and told her why a boy who could swim perfectly well did not try to save himself from drowning when he fell off that dratted roof and down into the murky water.

'Good idea,' Harry said, as if glad of something to do rather than just willing the half-conscious boy back to life.

They knelt one on each side of the tub, and the boy's sturdy little body still felt chilled under their urging hands, despite the warm water, the hot day and a fire. Viola and Harry massaged on and willed warmth and sense back into the suddenly fragile-seeming body. Bram's eyes opened to watch them as if it cost a huge effort, but at last Viola could see a spark of his usual life and spirit beginning to light them. She smiled a wobbly smile and knew it would break her heart if he could not breach the cold and shock and a nasty little head injury to come back to them more or less his old self from his watery ordeal.

How would his sisters and Harry feel if they lost him or his wits were impaired? No, she refused to even think of such outcomes. Except now they were in her head they would not go away. Hot tears scalded the backs of her eyes at the very idea of them all so overborne by grief again, and she had to blink them back and search for hope instead. Bram was all that mattered right now and he could not see her worst thoughts in her eyes. She saw the effort it was costing to force his way past the cold and shock, and knowing how fearful she was would not help him.

'You made a botched job of being a good boy this time, didn't you, love?' she said with a wobbly smile, and was it good that he had begun to shiver?

'In trouble?' he whispered past stiff-looking lips.

She shook her head frantically to hide these wretched tears, or shake them away so he would not notice them if that did not work. 'Not this time, though perhaps when you are feeling like your old self again, I might scold you for giving me such a terrible shock,' she amended, because if he got through this, she never wanted to fear for him so deeply again.

Sooner or later he must know what an ordeal this had been for the rest of them, but now they were all so intent on willing him to live that nothing else mattered. Today Bram had taught her what real fear was, and now she knew about it, she might never stop worrying about him ever again. Even if they were half a world apart and he hardly remembered she was his teacher decades ago, the bond would never break for her now she had let it catch hold. She loved these children; she let herself know how deeply as she willed Bram back to life with every ounce of steel she had in her.

She met Harry's intent gaze across the boy's head and saw her own fears and fierce love for the lad looking back at her. Never again would she be able to accuse him of being light-minded and irresponsible even in her head. Now she knew how deep his love for his wards was under the devil-may-care front he showed the wider world, she might never be able to fully defend herself against his powerful appeal to her senses ever again. As Bram became more like his old self, he finally noticed his terrified sisters were standing as close as they could get to the tub, as if they dare not take their eyes off him for fear he might expire.

'Sorry,' the boy murmured to them.

Harry flicked his gaze from Viola's down to his son of the spirit, then back again to hide his emotions from all three children as he looked as if his heart was about to break over that breathy but heart-felt apology as well.

'You will be if you don't get on and fight like a man,' he informed the lad with mock sternness to lighten the tense atmosphere for the children at least.

'Ah, that's good, well done,' the busy little local doctor said without a pause as he scurried into the bedchamber and only stopped to look down at his patient just in time not to stumble over the tub and join him in it. Viola tried to see what he would now and saw Bram's skin was pink again and life was coming back into the dark brown eyes his old nurse always said he got from his late father. 'Best wash all that mud and weed out of his hair while you have Master Bramford in there and keeping unusually still, Miss Yelverton,' the doctor observed, as if this had been an everyday mishap.

Even as she felt a certain sort of comfort in that idea, a small voice inside was asking, why her? Why was it a woman's work to wash the boy's hair and nobody else's? Not a question she expected or needed an answer to right now, but something told her Harry would have done it without a second thought if he had been first on the doctor's list of suitable hair washers instead of her.

'Can you run and find some soap for me, love?' she asked Emma and was glad when the girl nodded and went off to find it, Lucy still clinging to her big sister's hand as if she never intended to let go of the one sibling she could safely rely on to move heaven and earth not to leave her.

'A candle,' the doctor demanded, and Harry sprang up to get one before Viola could even ask what on earth for when the late summer sunlight was streaming in through the bank of leaded windows nearby. 'The shutters and a screen for the fire' was the next absent-minded order as the little man knelt down by the tub with the candlestick in his hand and took Harry's place there.

Viola reached out to hold Bram's hand and let him know she was here to support him while the doctor prodded for whatever he was prodding the poor lad for. When all was as dark in here as it could be in broad daylight, the doctor ordered Bram to watch the candle flame and closely observed his face and particularly his eyes as he waved it this way and that and the boy flinched from the light. Viola almost shouted at the man to stop making him feel even worse than he did already.

'Hmm, we shall see,' the doctor murmured almost to himself. Then he smiled at Bram as if he had done well, and of course he had, Viola thought militantly. He had not shouted or cried out or squirmed away, and she was not sure she would have been that brave after taking a blow on the head, then enduring the doctor's ministrations. The man turned his attention to ordering the available adults about next.

'You can open the door a touch and leave the shutters on that little window at the side of the room slightly ajar, but not fully open. That way you can all see what you are doing and Master Bramford will not have quite so much of a headache to endure as he would if we let too much light get into his eyes. I hate to think what you have been up to in order to land yourself in such a bumble broth this time, young man, but I suggest you never do it again,' he ended with an easy smile and a reassuring nod to the girls as they came running back into the room with a cake of scented soap Bram would normally not let anywhere near his manly skin, let alone the mop of wildly curling dark hair he already thought was annoyingly girlish and ought to be cropped into submission.

'It was in the lady's bedchamber,' Emma explained breathlessly and with a sidelong look at Harry, as if she knew she had been somewhere she ought not to go, but what else was she to do at a time like this?

'You did the right thing, little love, but now you have found some soap, you had best hand it over to Miss Yelverton, before your brother gets cold and decides he would rather smell of pond weed and mud than ancient rose petals and never mind what the rest of us think of his stink.'

Viola felt a little better when Bram wrinkled his nose slightly and squirmed under her soapy hands as she first cleaned his still grubby hands, then gently worked her way through his wet curls with lathered hands in order to tease out the last of the weed and slime without hurting his poor bruised forehead. To her, the finely milled soap smelt of summer and warm gardens and hope, but she thought she saw Harry flinch and turn away as if it whispered something very different to him. Intrigued now, she eyed him watchfully for a moment, then went back to her task. She held out an imperious hand for the cup thoughtful Emma was holding out so she could rinse the suds from the boy's hair without getting any in his eyes.

'There, you can stop your wriggling now, you ungrateful little toad, since I have finished trying to civilise you. At least the housekeeper will not be able to accuse us of ruining her good sheets with your mud and grime now,' she told Bram with a wry smile, and how wonderful it felt when he tried to slip away from her helping hands when she and Harry raised him out of the water very carefully between them and he suddenly became self-conscious about his state of nature.

'You could have sent the women away,' she heard Bram mutter reproachfully at Harry, even as he leaned on her arm as if his legs were a lot more wobbly than he wanted to admit.

'I think calling you a toad is a bit strong considering you are clean again, but Miss Yelverton does not look shocked by your ingratitude, which is quite an accomplishment, if you ask me. Now we had better put this towel under your head so Mrs Cartwright won't scold us and you for getting her best pillowcases wet,' Harry said cheerfully as they helped the boy into bed, for all the world as if he had no more fear for his ward and heir's health than if the boy had suddenly succumbed to a summer cold.

Viola saw the girls relax their tightly held bodies and knew Harry was right to make light of the fear he must still have about the darkness in this room and the doctor's slight frown as he watched the boy being put to bed as if he had half a dozen eggs stuffed in his non-existent pockets and they did not want to break a single one of them.

'Do the girls have to watch? I haven't got a stitch on.' Bram murmured a boy's protest that nearly had Viola cheering, even if Emma and Lucy looked offended by his attack of manly modesty.

'That will shortly be the least of our worries, young man. If I am not very much mistaken, someone has woken your Great-Aunt Tam and given her the glad news about your adventures. From the sound of it, she is on her way upstairs to find out what you have been up to, so I would hop into bed and pretend you are asleep, if I were you,' Harry said with a rueful look at Bram, then Viola, as if there was not much he could do to stop a force of nature.

'Oh, no,' Lucy gasped out, then slapped her free hand over her mouth as she heard herself being very rude about her great-aunt, and Viola could not rebuke her for saying what they were all thinking.

'Why did you let me sleep through all the fuss and flapping, my girl?' the lady barked at Viola as she bustled into the room and cast a hasty look at Bram, who had at least scrambled into bed and drawn up the bedclothes in time to hide his nakedness from his fiercest critic. 'Why was I not told immediately?' Miss Marbeck demanded when nobody answered her first question.

Viola knew her fearsome glare was caused by

nine parts fear to one part fury, but Bram and the girls were paler than ever at the sight of it, and Viola wished the lady would find another way of venting her anxiety for her beloved great-nephew or go away.

'I expect they were all too busy rescuing this young man and finding me, ma'am,' the doctor said bravely.

'I dare say; some fool is always fancying themselves ill when they should know you are going to be needed by silly boys who fall from one scrape into the next without as much as a thought for the rest of us.'

Viola caught a glimpse of real exasperation in Harry's blue eyes and stepped nobly into the breach in her turn, before he said something he would regret when he was feeling more like himself.

'Perhaps we two could take the girls downstairs now Bram is safely in bed and looking more like his old self again, Miss Marbeck. Lucy and Emma are the only ones who can tell you exactly what happened since I was not there and neither was Sir Harry. The doctor needs to make sure Bram is in rude health again, then talk to his guardian about fitting him with a ball and chain to stop him from doing it again, whatever it was,' she said, with a mock stern look for her pupil and a warning look for Miss Marbeck to say the children had suffered enough of a shock today and scolding them to hide her own fears would not help. She knew that the lady cared deeply for these orphans and had changed her whole way of life for them, but Miss Marbeck was never going to be the kind of great-aunt who would hug or soothe her nieces as they probably needed to be hugged and soothed at the moment.

'Maybe we could do that,' the lady said with a challenging glare at her great-nephew to say he had the girls' obvious distress to thank for him getting away with this latest piece of mischief, whatever it might have been.

She swept regally out of the room with an irritated sniff and left Viola to trail along behind her, holding the girls' hands to let them know she was certainly not angry with them. At least Lucy had finally relaxed her frantic grip on her big sister's hand in her awe at her great-aunt's fury. Perhaps it was as well the little girl had no idea the lady had been so worried about Bram that her anger was a way of covering up her acute anxiety about him. Viola gave Lucy's hand a reassuring squeeze and rolled her eyes at the lady's back to silently say the lady's mood was unpredictable, but nothing for her to worry about. This was an exceptional day and Miss Yelverton could take a short holiday while Viola did any hugging and soothing the girls needed.

'If a body could die of shock and worry, I would have done it over that young limb of Satan you two call a brother the moment I found out the boy did his best to drown himself as soon as my back was turned,' the lady said irritably and confirmed Viola's suspicions as they went down the stairs.

The lady was fearful of losing any more of her family, but she walked as sternly upright as ever as she led the way across the grand entrance hall, even if she did go more slowly after the effort of getting upstairs to Bram as fast as her legs would carry her must have cost more than she was willing to admit.

Bram had taught Viola a valuable lesson in looking deeper into the feelings and hidden places of this family's hearts. Nothing was as simple as she had thought when she was on her way here and counting up the days and weeks and months until she could go back to her old life and leave most of them behind. Miss Marbeck was seventy if she was a day and the ups and downs of caring about three enterprising young children looked hard on her today.

Harry was as strong and protective and caring as any man could be about his wards, but even he had his secret fears for their welfare. Perhaps that was what made him spoil them when Viola thought they needed more boundaries in their lives to stop this sort of thing happening again. Emma and maybe even Lucy would worry about their reckless brother all the time if they were not careful.

Suddenly those six months she had been wishing away did not look as set in stone as they had only a few hours ago, and that was before Harry kissed her, she reminded herself with a frown to stop herself dreaming of it like a besotted girl. Her first passionate, fully engaged with and longed-for kiss ought to have changed everything for both of them instead of just for her. Somehow her knowing about the real and complex Sir Harry under the dare-anything, apparently fearless front probably did not change anything for him while her whole world felt under threat.

Chapter Nine

'I am in no need of help, young woman. I am not an invalid,' Miss Marbeck informed Viola stiffly.

'No, ma'am, of course you do not and are not.'

'Impudent girl and you are not to linger down here with my scallywag of a nephew now I am going to my bed.'

'So I cannot come upstairs with you, but I must not stay downstairs either. You have set me quite a challenge, Miss Marbeck.'

'Pah! I have no idea what I did to deserve a family like this one, and you should stop bothering me with your chopped logic and let me go to bed in peace.'

'I am not standing in your way,' Viola pointed out, only staying here at the bottom of the stairs because she knew any attempt to go up them with her gruff chaperon would be seen as a sign that she thought Miss Marbeck was entering her dotage. Or at least that was what she told herself as she stood at Sir Harry's side, watching the lady go her weary way upstairs, and heard him stifle a sigh at his aunt's contrariness.

'Thank you,' he said as soon as they heard the door of the bedchamber his aunt had been given for the night close sharply behind her. 'Aunt Tam is terrified history will repeat itself under all the bravado and bluster.'

'I know,' Viola replied and felt guilty about the shiver of sensual awareness wriggling down her backbone because they were down here alone, even if it would only be for the few brief minutes they had before Miss Marbeck stuck her head out of her bedchamber door to demand why Viola was still down here or sent someone down to find out what they were doing. His closeness and the flutter in her heart because he had shown her so much of the real man under the disguise today was not very good at remembering this was a short and never-to-be-repeated interlude.

'So am I,' he added so softly she could not have heard if she was a sensible further step away, or so she told herself as she refused to put it between them even now.

'I know the doctor said we must keep a close eye on Bram and make sure he stays in bed for at least another day, but from the way he was demanding food and something to do when he woke up tonight, I think we can safely say he is almost back to his usual self,' she said.

Harry had always been so strong and self-assured, she knew in her heart he did not need her to tell him that. Of course she would be able to leave at the end of her two years without him feeling more than a fleeting moment of regret. Yet when it came to the children and his aunt, he was vulnerable to all the usual worries about their health and happiness. No wonder he wanted to share some of them with a sympathetic listener after a shock like the one Bram gave them all today.

'Let us hope he has learned something from his latest scrape, since I doubt *my* heart will stand too many days like this one, let alone Aunt Tam's,' Harry said with a preoccupied frown as they stood side by side, like an old married couple discussing an exhausting day and too weary to face climbing the stairs to bed yet.

That picture of happily wedded contentment would never be reality and Viola made herself face facts. She and Sir Harry Marbeck were as distant from each other as the earth and the moon. They would stay that way and never mind that kiss in the library before Bram brought the true state of affairs home to both of them once again. They both had responsibilities that forbade furtive kisses when nobody else was looking.

'When I smelt the soap you were using on Bram's hair this afternoon, I suddenly remembered how my mother always used to smell of roses,' he said, as if he was still so lost in memory he had forgotten she was his wards' governess and he was telling her such a personal thing.

Viola eyed him warily, but he looked as if he was

still lost in a newly triggered childhood memory, so she said nothing and waited to see if there was anything more he wanted to tell her.

'She must have used rosewater as well as rose-scented soap, as if she wanted to smell of summer to help her keep my father's wintery coldness at bay. Of course I was only a small boy back then and did not understand such adult matters, but I caught a waft of her special scent when you were soaping Bram and it reminded me of her. As a small boy, I thought of her as somehow always warm and summery and loving; while he was just a strange man who did not like me much. That last bit turned out to be true, by the way,' he ended with a wry grin, as if recovering his adult persona of not caring about anything deeply and his parents' failed marriage least of all.

'Maybe the first part is as well, then,' she could not stop herself saying even as she saw the polite mask come down over his handsome features, as if he did not want his newly recovered memories to argue with his mother's heartless desertion of her only child. Viola should not want to fight for his softer memories of his mother either, nor want to make him feel better about his stark childhood after the woman left him alone with his harsh father. She was far too aware of his moods and expressions already, and wanting him to be happier about the past was a step further into the trap of caring too much about this unattainable, unknowable man.

'Children seldom have the judgement to see a situation as it really is, especially at the age you were when your mother left. Adults put their own gloss on events and children are too young to question it,' she said carefully, holding her breath in the hope he would say more about his mother and perhaps begin to let the yawning gap there must have been in his young life when Lady Marbeck left her husband for another man heal over at last.

'My father was not the sort to polish a bare and stony fact so I could feel better about it, Miss Yelverton,' he said briskly and suddenly seemed to have noticed that they were alone down here and it was high time they were not. Disappointed that he refused to even try to understand himself and his past better, she turned away from him with a hasty goodnight. She refused to look back to see if he thought her abrupt or rude as she went upstairs.

Of course she was not angry with the man for shutting her out of his thoughts so abruptly and as if they had never shared that kiss or a few private moments together after such an eventful day. He could brood on his parents' disastrous marriage and his lonely childhood all night long, for all she cared. She had Lucy and Emma to worry about and Bram to check up on every time she was awake and restless in the night. Or she would have, if his guardian had not decided it was his job to sit by Bram's bed tonight, in case he woke up and needed reassurance or took a turn for the worse. Viola sighed and wished she had brought a book upstairs to read as she faced the ordeal of somehow whiling away a long night in between restless bouts of sleep and this terrible longing for so many things she would never have.

Harry started awake in his chair and listened to Bram mutter in his sleep, then settle again. It felt as if he had only just dropped off and he drew his elegant gold watch out of his waistcoat pocket and held it up to the shielded candlelight. Two o'clock in the morning and about as dead an hour as anyone should sleep through, even at this time of year when dawn was not quite as far away as it would be in a few months' time. He recalled waking up on nights like this as a boy and knowing he had to lie there still and quiet since his father had given orders the boy was not to be indulged and any crying or wailing must be punished.

Now that a memory of his mother had whispered under his guard, he let himself remember how she used to insist he was close enough for her to hear him if he cried out in the night. It was only after she left them that his father had Harry banished to the top of the house and the echoing old nurseries he had ruled over himself as the eldest boy and heir. It was almost as if the old man thought it was his son's fault she had gone, but now Harry had let an adult view of the past shine into places he had locked away all these years he wondered if old Sir Alfred had been whistling in the dark.

If the man had any feelings at all, and Harry had often doubted it, had he been striking at the only bit of his wife left by treating her son as if he was the spawn of the devil? Harry watched Bram sleep with a love so deep for the boy it almost hurt and a feeling that his sire had been even more childish and hateful than he'd thought if that was truly how he had thought of his only child.

How could a father do that to his own son when he felt such protective love for this boy who was not even his? Thank God the old man was dead now so he could not even try to interfere in the children's upbringing. Chris would never have left his children in the old man's harsh care after rescuing Harry from him as a boy. His cousin would never have risked such hard neglect for his own children just for the sake of respecting the head of a family who had done nothing to deserve it. Harry wondered whom Chris and Jane had named as guardian for their children before Harry was of age and almost laughed out loud as he suddenly knew it would have been Aunt Tam. The old man would have been even closer to an apoplexy from sheer bad temper than usual if he had ever discovered that insult to his manly superiority.

Harry sat at Bram's bedside and was very glad to conclude his late father had been quite right—he *did* take after his faithless, heartless and light-minded mother, thank heaven, because he would hate to think he had the bad taste to follow Sir Alfred Marbeck's example. Did that make him the echo of Sir Alfred's unflattering picture of his wife in nature as well as looks? Hard to tell when her hasty departure robbed him of all but the most fugitive memory of her. Suddenly he wished he had not put the letter his late mother's lover sent him after her death straight on the fire, so he had another side to her story even if he did only believe part of it. When he realised she was not coming back, he had shut all thought of her in a dark cupboard and done his best to pretend she did not exist, but now it felt as if he had to know more about her to be a whole man.

The part of him that had refused to grow up fully and face the real world reeled when the care of Christian and Jane's children fell on him. The man who he seemed to be growing into knew that sooner or later he would have to face once having been a lost and lonely boy whose mother had left him with a father who hated him when she decided her lover was more important to her than her son. He could not go on skating on the surface of life now he had the children to care for and get to adulthood without them suffering more trauma than they had already suffered.

Here he was, half wishing Miss Yelverton was at the end of that two-year promise he had made her sign and she could go back to Bath and stop torturing him with feral longings for her. And what about the other half? Better not think about what that part of him really wanted of her when she was only a few yards away along the corridor, with Emma and Lucy innocently asleep in the little room off the big one Miss Yelverton had been given for that very reason. So she might as well be in Bath, for all the good they could be to one another tonight as lovers.

He stifled a groan in deference to Bram's slumbers, even if he looked as if the last trump would hardly be loud enough to wake him up after his busy day. Harry knew he could never be the ready for any lark, daredevil, raffish man about town he had once been ever again. That Harry did not fit this new life, but he really did need to find himself another mistress so he would be able to keep his hands off a lady who would have every right to expect more from him than a happy tumble and a few luxurious trinkets to say thank you for sating his most urgent needs and desires.

Yet such careless sensuality seemed wrong now he had a family and a governess to consider. He would squirm every time Miss Yelverton cast her steely gaze over his unsatisfactory person and she did not even know that he was on the hunt for a woman to sate his baser desires with and keep him from lusting after her. Yet why did such a practical solution to his fascination with her seem low and impossible even to him as he thought about the gap Glory had left in his bed when she decided she had endured enough of country living?

'Uncle Harry, why are you here?' Bram opened his eyes and asked sleepily, and Harry could have kissed the boy if they were not both so manly it was unthinkable.

'Who knows, brat?' he replied with a grin and set about settling the boy back to sleep with a sigh of relief. He had sailed into some very choppy waters today and, as long as he avoided thinking about his mother and Miss Yelverton from now on, he might manage to avoid drowning in them yet.

Chapter Ten

A week later Viola snatched a weary moment to yearn for the night of brief naps and restless dreams she endured that first night at Chantry Old Hall so she could use it for its proper purpose and sleep like a baby. They had been about to leave the next day, after a spirited argument with Bram about him staying where he was until the doctor declared him fit to travel home, when Lucy was violently sick. Coping with a crying child and all the mess, as well as a bevy of flustered maids with mops, then ordering a bath for poor Lucy this time, Viola had put her hand on the little girl's forehead and found it hot as the stones in the still relentless heat from the sun.

'Oh, you poor love, we will get you nice and clean and comfortable again. Then perhaps you had best go back to bed for a while so you can sleep and wake up feeling more like your old self again,' she had said that long, weary week ago, as if she really thought it was only overexcitement and yesterday's upset

that caused the little girl's sickness. Her heart had
thumped with dread when she eyed the hard flush
of colour on Lucy's piquant little face and knew it
was far more than that.

'Please go and find your Uncle Harry for me,
Emma,' she had forced herself to say calmly. 'Tell
him I would like to see him as soon as he has a moment to spare. Then go and find Nanny and tell her
we cannot leave just yet and she will be needed upstairs for a while.'

Emma had eyed her little sister anxiously, as if
she did not quite believe that comfortable version of
events either, and sped off to do as she was bid. At
the time Viola took a moment to worry about the ef-
fect yet another dose of fear would have on the poor
girl, but then Lucy had burst into unhappy tears and
diverted Viola from one worry to a more acute one
of what could really be the matter with the youngest Marbeck.

'What is it?' Harry had demanded as he strode
into the bedroom where the girls had slept the night
before.

'Lucy does not feel very well, Sir Harry,' she had
told him with a stern glare to tell him not to let out his
true feelings as she stood aside to let him see Lucy,
now clean and in yesterday's not-quite-as-clean shift,
since there had seemed no point in sending down to
Garrard House for her nightgown when she was only
supposed to be staying here for one night.

'I was very sick, Uncle Harry,' the little girl told
him mournfully.

'Were you, my Lucy? I expect your mouth still tastes horrid, then.'

'Yes, and it hurts.'

'Here, then, my love. Sip some more water to take the taste away, and as soon as Nanny gets here to look after you, I will go down to the kitchen and find you something to make it feel better,' Viola recalled saying, as if she really thought that was all they would need to do the trick.

If only, she thought now as weariness sat on her like a soggy blanket in this humid air. This heatwave seemed to be going on and on, and the humidity made all their lives more difficult. They had tried so hard to stop Bram and Emma catching scarlet fever from their little sister, and goodness knew where she had got it from in the first place. Great-Aunt Tam had whisked Bram back to Garrard House in order to isolate him from the infection and, although it was a childhood illness, Viola did not blame Harry for stressing the need for someone to keep a close eye on Bram in order to persuade his aunt to stay down there as well. At least the daily accounts Miss Marbeck sent up to Chantry Old Hall of Bram's continuing rude health and the fact his restlessness was driving her demented said they were both well, but poor little Emma had not been so lucky.

At least that meant the girls could now be nursed in the same room and Viola was saved a long trek from this slip of a room off her own up to the one in the old nurseries where Emma had slept until it became obvious she had already caught the illness from her little sister. Lucy was now sleeping in a little bed Sir Harry's estate carpenters had made her as soon as Emma became ill as well and they needed their own spaces to be sore and fretful in. At least sharing Lucy's sickroom would stop Emma worrying about her little sister's health far more than her own. Viola frowned and met Harry's worried eyes as he sat holding Emma's hot little hand. It was clear to both of them that Emma was the one they must fret about now, as Lucy improved every day and her sore throat and itchy rash had always been less severe than her big sister's.

Emma seemed to have caught a far worse dose of the infection and was in a high fever. Nanny had proved to be more of a hindrance than a help in the sickroom, since she insisted on believing the worst. She muttered not quite quietly enough about a family curse and bewailed her poor, dear Master Christian's untimely end, which made Emma miss her beloved mama and papa more than ever and cry as if her poor heart might break.

Viola was glad Harry soon saw the woman was too old and gloomy for even the lesser role she played in the children's lives now that even Lucy was almost a young lady. Of course Harry had kept the elderly woman on even after she began to tire easily and look on the dark side of everything more than usual. He must have felt he had to keep things as safe and familiar as he could for the children when their parents died. In Viola's opinion, it was time Nanny retired and thought the worst in peace, as she deserved to after a lifetime of service to Christian Marbeck and his father before him.

Now Nanny had been banished from the sick-room, never mind propriety and any gossip because Viola was on her own in here with Harry. Emma and Lucy were soothed by his patience and good humour, and he and Viola were far too busy nursing two sick children at the same time to have a spare moment for misbehaving. Right now it felt like a shame they could not exchange a hug or a quick kiss to comfort one another as their anxiety over Emma's illness haunted them both, but at least he was here and she did not have to face the fear on her own.

The heat of the day limped on into a sticky night, and the thought of either of them seeking their beds as Emma grew ever hotter and more restless in hers felt unthinkable. Even sponging the poor girl down with cold water and persuading her to drink as often as they could coax her into doing so did not seem to bring her temperature down for very long.

Eventually Emma became so restless and fever-ish she kept waking Lucy up with her moans and thrashing about, looking for a cool spot on her pil-low, that Viola and Harry decided he would carry Lucy into the other room and put her into Viola's bed to sleep in peace. There was little chance Viola would occupy it tonight, and it made sense for Lucy to be near enough for them to hear her if she called out, but far enough away not to be disturbed by her sister's nightmares and muttered complaints in her rare moments of lucidity.

* * *

Hours went by with Emma growing less and less like her usual patient self as she tossed and turned fretfully and even pushed Viola away when she tried to rub the soothing ointment from the doctor on to her sore and itchy skin. If not for Harry's steadfast strength when they had to strip the girl of her night-gown and wash her with water cold from the well, Viola thought she might have broken down and cried, too. She hated seeing brave and patient Emma brought so low by this wretched fever she was out of her senses most of the time now.

Viola was so afraid for this dear, serious-minded girl when it began to feel as if nothing they could do would help her and the night was so hot and endless it made everything seem even worse. She felt a little bit lost herself in the sticky half-dark of this lamplit room and knew she might have despaired if not for Harry's steadfast presence.

'Perhaps we should close the windows,' she murmured as they hastily covered Emma's shivering body with a sheet and blankets when all that fever-ish heat seemed to leach out of her all of a sudden and they faced the opposite problem of trying to get her warm again.

'You know it was stuffy and airless in here until we opened them and it seemed as if she could hardly breathe.'

'I know you are right, but it feels as if there really is a storm waiting to make things worse out there tonight,' she said and shook her head at her own folly. The weather hardly seemed to matter as they battled a far worse problem than a little too much humidity and tension in the air on such a sticky night. 'She is sweating again,' she added with an agonised look, as if to say what on earth was left for them to do to try to help this loving and wonderful child they had not already done?

'Help me lift her up, then. We should probably change the sheets again to try to make her feel drier and a little more comfortable.'

'Of course, I should have thought of that. Will you hold her while I strip the bed then make it up again? She seems to know it is you holding her even when she is wandering in her mind about everything else.'

'I probably sound a bit like Chris,' he said, and Viola saw the terror she shared for this precious girl in his eyes as they exchanged glances over the top of Emma's dark head and remembered why her father and mother were not here instead of wild Sir Harry and the governess.

'Or maybe you sound like yourself,' she argued. Harry always thought he was less than the excellent guardian she knew him to be after all these months waiting for him to grow bored with being one and get back to his old life of daredevilry and pleasure seeking. Now she knew he would never leave the children alone and unanchored, as he must have felt for most of his childhood and early youth. And he needed to know the children loved him for his own sake and not any fugitive resemblance he had to his late cousin.

'Emma loves *you*, Sir Harry,' she added in case that
was too subtle a hint to get past his skewed view of
himself as unworthy of affection.

'She certainly adores you,' he murmured back.

There was the fly in the ointment she must think
about when Emma was better again, as she simply
had to be, because the idea of living without her felt
utterly bleak. Viola did not think Harry or Miss Marbeck or the other two children could endure any more
sorrow and she certainly did not want to learn how
it was done. But if this dearly loved girl recovered,
how could Viola leave her the moment her promised
two years were up, as if she and her brother and sister did not matter?

Trying not to think about the answer to that question for the sake of her own sanity when Harry was
so close and so, well, important to her somehow, she
bustled about stripping the bed and fetching clean
sheets from the ancient press in the corner where the
housekeeper had left piles of them ready for when
they were needed. Action helped; anything that might
bring this suddenly fragile girl some relief made an
even better distraction.

While she did all that as fast and efficiently as she
could with shaking hands, Harry held Emma in his
arms and crooned a senseless sort of lullaby to her
that almost made Viola smile. He was clearly making use of whatever words came into his head, and
it was the rumble of his deep voice that calmed Emma's feverish ramblings as if she was listening to it
and finding some comfort.

A faint rumble of thunder in the distance made Viola pause in the act of shaking the top sheet into place and meet Harry's eyes with a question in her own. Perhaps this time the weather really was breaking and the sticky heat of the last few days would abate at long last. He nodded to say he had heard it, too. Knowing what the other was thinking might feel dangerous to both of them at any other time, but tonight it gave her a light layer of comfort in what felt like an otherwise comfortless situation.

'There we are, my love. All clean and neat again for you to get back into,' she told Emma softly as soon as she had finished and gone back to Harry's side so she could peer down at Emma, who now had her eyes half-open, but there was a faraway look in them. She looked vaguely in the direction of the clean bed awaiting her, as if it felt too lonely to be desirable, clean or not.

'No. I want you, Uncle Harry,' Emma demanded the moment he moved to get up and put her back into bed. 'Don't let me go.'

He relaxed his half-standing stance and sat back down with the child in his arms and a helpless look for Viola to say what else could he do but sit here with Emma if that was what she really wanted?

'My shawl should be soft enough not to make her itch if we can get it around her and, as being held by you obviously makes her feel better, why not?' Viola said and slipped back into the other bedroom to snatch a quick look at Lucy, who was sleeping like a baby, before she hunted for her best Norwich shawl she had brought with her all those days ago for some odd reason that escaped her now. She was glad she must have thought she needed another layer to hide behind back then, even if it had been too hot to wear it, and she sped back to the smaller room with it. At Harry's nod, she did her best to tuck Emma up in its warm softness, despite her struggles to throw it off again.

'No, Sprat, you must have something around you whether you like it or not, even if you are feeling much too hot to want it,' Harry told the feverish girl in his arms as Emma weakly tried to bat Viola's hands away.

'Rock her,' Viola ordered. 'And this time I will do the singing.'

'You certainly cannot be any worse at it than I am,' he said as he settled back in his chair and gathered Emma close again as soon as she was covered up. At least she had given up trying to push the shawl aside.

Then he did as Viola asked him to and rocked the girl as gently as if she was a fractious baby. Remembering as many silly songs as she could drag up from memories of her childhood, Viola tried to only make a gentle background noise that would distract Emma from the thunder rolling ever closer outside. She prayed silently that Lucy would sleep through the noise and lightning flashes beginning to light up the night so they could concentrate all their efforts on soothing Emma into any sort of sleep that might give her a respite from this endless tossing and turning.

'She is going cold again,' Harry said rather desperately as that wild light outside shone briefly through the gap between the shutters Viola had hastily closed against it and a great crack of thunder broke overhead.

'Here, I can wrap her up in this blanket as well if you can manage to shift her without waking her up,' Viola whispered. At any other time, being so close to the man would have sent her silly body into paroxysms of pure joy, but now it only managed an excited hum to remind her how much of a man he was while they worried over his eldest ward.

'There now, my lovely,' he soothed Emma as she stirred and seemed about to protest against whatever they were doing to her this time. 'If you are quiet and keep still while Miss Yelverton looks after you, I will tell you all about Bad Sir Toby Marbeck and his dashing adventures as a buccaneer on the Spanish Main.'

'Sir Toby?' Emma asked, and Viola could have cheered at that sign of interest in anything but this wretched fever that was racking what suddenly seemed such a touchingly small body under the new layer of wrappings.

'Yes. Has nobody ever told you about him?'

'No,' Emma said and put her thumb in her mouth as if she was back in her nursery again.

Harry began an imaginative tale about a Sir Toby he had probably just made up, and Viola listened out for Lucy's call after yet another terrific clap of thunder, but still she heard nothing and marvelled at the little girl's ability to sleep through so much noise when every one of her big sister's murmurings had woken her earlier tonight. It felt incredible to find her own eyes were so heavy that she had to fight off sleep as Harry softened his voice and slowed his story even as the storm outside worked its way to a furious crescendo.

Viola snapped wide awake when some ancient tree crashed to the ground out in the park after the latest dazzling flash of lightning and a great boom of thunder felt so close she could taste the sulphurous aftermath in the tense stillness outside. She ran over just in time to push open the shutters and close the open window as the first heavy drops of rain began to plop against it. Then the spots became a mighty downpour that hammered against the panes as if Mother Nature herself was hell-bent on coming inside this ancient old place tonight to find out what the mere humans within it were about.

'At least the air feels a lot cooler now,' she said softly and listened to the thunder rolling off into the distance and the drum of rain on the diamond-paned windows. The house felt safe and protective, despite all the disasters that had happened since they'd arrived here for a summer picnic more than a week ago now. Viola returned to the empty fireside and sat on the bed, since she could not bear to return to her chair on the opposite side of it now that felt too far away from Emma and Harry.

Harry put a finger to his lips and nodded silently at Emma sleeping in his arms. 'She is as well,' he whispered, and Viola felt tears sting her eyes as he returned his attention to his eldest ward as if he could hardly believe Emma's fever had broken at long last.

'Oh, thank God,' Viola murmured as she let herself believe he was right. This time Emma was truly asleep and not wandering in feverish half-dreams as she had been for most of yesterday and up to this very early morning as they listened to the rain outside and watched her sleep.

Now she had begun it, Emma's sleep seemed so deep and determined Harry could lay her back in her bed and return to his chair by the side of it without her as much as stirring. Viola went to her chair on the opposite side from him without any sign of their patient waking and blessed the man for not ordering her off to the neighbouring room to share her bed with Lucy when she would not sleep a wink and might disturb the little girl with her restless need to know for certain that Emma was still asleep and not feverish again.

She liked to think she loved all three children equally, and Lucy had certainly charmed her way into Viola's heart these last eighteen months along with her enterprising brother, but Emma would always be special. She was the child who had tugged at Viola's heartstrings from the day she walked into her classroom looking worried and homesick and doing her best to pretend she was perfectly all right and nobody needed to worry about her. Even before she was orphaned, Emma brought out something in Viola she had not really wanted to know she had until she met the girl. This family, she decided with half-hearted exasperation, had a way of pushing themselves into corners of her mind she did not want to let anyone else into, whether she wanted them there or not.

Chapter Eleven

Despite the doctor's assurances that scarlet fever was rarely catching for very long after a patient's fever broke, it was another week before they dared to reunite the children. It had simply felt like too much of a risk until then after their dreadful fright about Emma, so it was September now and a nice enough day for the time of year when Bram was finally allowed up the hill to meet his sisters and help his great-aunt bring them back home again. At least it was not as punishingly hot as it had been when they travelled up the hill to Chantry Old Hall that first day without the slightest inkling it would be so long before they could all go back home again.

'There you see, boy—your sisters are alive and well just as I told you they would be. Now maybe you will stop fretting and fidgeting and believe your elders and betters in future,' Miss Marbeck told Bram as he tumbled out of the barouche and rushed up to his sisters, then stopped and remembered he was far too old and manly to hug them, so he nodded solemnly at each of them in turn and told them he was very pleased to see them well again.

'We missed you,' Lucy admitted briefly and with a look of almost comical surprise on her face. 'But come and see the books Uncle Harry got for us in Oxford, Bram. Miss Yelverton says we can share the atlas and you can have the adventure stories, but the animal book is all mine,' Lucy told her brother, then ran after him in case he chose to ignore her declaration of ownership.

'I had better go with them or they will fight,' Emma said with a sigh, and she left Viola, Harry and Miss Marbeck standing on the carriageway trying to pretend they were not delighted that life was back to normal again at last and all three children seemed back to their usual selves.

'The girls look well enough. I dare say it was a storm in a teacup,' Miss Marbeck said gruffly. If Viola could not see through her brusque manner to the anxiety underneath it, she might have run after the children and left Harry to deal with his crossgrained aunt alone.

'And you and Bram have obviously not killed one another while we were worrying ourselves unduly over his sisters, Auntie Dear,' Harry observed sardonically.

'One more day incarcerated down there together and we might well have done. That boy is nothing but a rogue in the making.'

'And you dote on him.'

'I do nothing of the kind; I could hardly wait to be rid of him today, if the truth be known.'

'And isn't that a rare commodity around here?' Harry said with his eyebrows raised at his aunt's tetchy lie and his tongue firmly in his cheek.

'True, my boy,' the lady said blandly, 'and what have you two been up to while I was trying my patience to the limit down at Garrard House over that ungrateful young cub?'

'Looking after your great-nieces for you,' Harry responded, and Viola was glad she could fade into the background after all, intending to leave him to give battle as soon as she could slide away without them noticing.

'Every moment of the day for nigh on a fortnight?' his aunt asked with a sly glance from Sir Harry to Viola, which she did not like the look of one little bit. She was in enough trouble without any sly suspicions from the woman she had thought she could trust to see how unsuitable a match it would be, even if either of them had the slightest intention of making it.

'Have you any idea how hard it is to keep two girls amused, but not racing about and overtiring themselves while they are being kept busy, Aunt Tam?'

'Yes, but I admit I am surprised you do as well.'

'Then you can be sure we have both been fully occupied ever since they felt well enough to need amusing.'

'Not both of you together, I hope.'

'Please don't play the high stickler now, Aunt Tam.

Neither of us have the staying power for it after the last two weeks.'

'Hmm, I suppose that housekeeper of yours slept close by to make sure Miss Yelverton's good name could not be blown on by the gossips?'

'Of course she did and the gossips can go hang anyway.'

'That would probably stop them looking for the worst interpretation of every story they pried into as if they have a right, but I doubt if anything else ever will,' the lady pointed out, as if they needed reminding.

Viola flushed and did her best not to meet Sir Harry's eyes as she recalled their heady kiss that first day here when Miss Marbeck herself slept on, oblivious to a potential scandal under her very nose. 'There is nothing for anyone to gossip about,' she said anyway. 'We all had to stay here until we were quite sure Bram would not catch the fever from his sisters. I do not care what stories anyone makes up about it. We could not take any risks with him after he fell in the lake and was so lucky to have been pulled out alive.'

'Pray do not remind me. I swear he took ten years off my life that day and I don't have that many to spare,' Miss Marbeck said with a shudder and let the subject of Sir Harry's and Viola's reputations drop.

Viola thought it would be odd to spend a day at Chantry Old Hall as if nothing much had happened since the last time they were all here together, but instead it turned out to be all the things the first one was meant to be—without the kiss, of course, which did seem a pity to her wild side now there was no need to worry about the children for one minute out of every two. Thank goodness the air was fresher since the storm the night Emma turned the corner and came back to them. The oldest and mightiest oak in Harry's park had been struck down as if one life had been required that night and thank God it was that one. They strolled over to look at the sad wreckage of a grand old tree that could have been a sapling when the Normans invaded Britain and must have already been a fine broad specimen when the house was built. Even Bram was awed by the height and breadth of the ruined tree and the effort it would take to get it chopped up and all the brash cleared away.

'It's only three months and two weeks until Christmas, so can we use it as the Yule log, Uncle Harry?' Lucy asked eagerly while Viola did some frantic calculations and realised the first week of September had passed without her taking much notice of it.

'Oh, no! Is that truly the date?' she said out loud as soon as she tracked it back to when they came, then put her hands over her mouth and stared wide-eyed at Harry as if he might be able to change it if he tried hard enough.

'Well, yes, but what of it?'

'I am going to miss my brother's wedding,' she gasped out, the wrongness of not being there for Darius on his wedding day tipping her over into tears. She was horrified to feel them form, then fall, so no wonder Harry looked as if he would rather be

fifty miles away. She had managed to keep them
under control through all the trials of the last week
and more—now she was turning into a watering pot.
'Darius's wedding,' she added, as if he would understand when he did not even know who Darius was.
Dignity and coolness in a crisis could go hang for
once because she was about to let her brother down
yet again. And her sister, Marianne, would take her
absence as a sure sign Viola did not care a snap of
her fingers for either of her siblings and be deeply
hurt Viola had not even made an effort to attend.

'When is it?' Harry demanded, as if it had to matter if she was going to cry about it, and that only
made her do it all the more.

'Tomorrow, at eleven o'clock,' she said tragically.
Of course there was no chance of getting there unless she grew wings or borrowed a fast horse and
rode there. 'Dulcimer!' she exclaimed with the frantic
eagerness of the desperate. 'Can I borrow her?' she
asked, staring at him with pleading eyes she knew
were still swimming with tears because she was
doing her best to brush them away with her fingers,
and what a terrible example that was to the children.

'I presume your brother can get married without
you and I expect he and his bride will be pleased to
see you as soon as you can get there by more conven-
tional methods,' he said in such a reasonable voice
she wanted to slap him for an awful moment, 'especially when you explain the very good reason why
you could not get there in time for the wedding.'

'You don't understand,' she told him and waved an agitated hand as if it might say more than she could.

'Come along, children,' Miss Marbeck said after a considering look at Viola and one at Harry to say he was on his own with this undone version of the children's governess she did not recognise either. 'I want proper sums for how much that monster weighed, and it will take all three of you to pace out and measure the length, breadth and circumference of it.'

Intrigued by the idea, and already bored by talk of people they had never met, the children happily scampered off to clamber around the fallen giant and shout numbers out until they lost interest and simply played in its shadows and built new adventures among its hoary old branches.

Grateful for Miss Marbeck's unexpected attack of tact, Viola searched for the right words to convince Harry how much it mattered for her to be there for Darius and his Fliss as well as for Marianne tomorrow, if there was any chance she could get to Owlet Manor in time.

'Why does it matter so much?' he asked, as if the day looked festive, but not important to an outsider.

How could she explain to a man who had no brothers and sisters and whose parents must have been as estranged as they could possibly be without actually killing one another? She searched for enough calm to reason herself around to his point of view, but she just could not manage it. 'It is important,' she said and turned away from him to thump the air in frustration—how could she persuade him it was when she was not quite sure why it felt so urgent for her to be there herself? 'Because I have not behaved well towards my brother and sister in the past,' she finally admitted.

He just grinned at her, drat him. 'Oh, surely not,' he said facetiously and even managed to look delighted that stern and steely Miss Yelverton might not be such a pattern card as she pretended. He already knew it was pretend after she had ridden like a hoyden across this very park on the day Bram terrified the propriety out of her by falling in the lake.

'Stop laughing at me. This is serious,' she demanded, as if she had the right to, and common sense whispered she did not.

'But you always behave properly; it is very humbling for the rest of us and sometimes a little bit annoying as well,' he said, as if enjoying her admission she was not perfect too much to let her off lightly, and what a good thing he had no idea how imperfect she really was.

'Well, I have not done so towards my family,' she admitted crossly. 'And you must have realised after that ride the other day that I was once a tomboy and quite defiant and wayward with it.'

'The idea had crossed my mind,' he admitted with an unholy grin to say he treasured the notion and intended to use it against her whenever the need arose from now on. 'And how I would have loved to have met you in your unregenerate state, Miss Yelverton,' he added with a wicked smile to let her know that glimpse of her legs the other day had whetted his rakish appetites even more than their scandalous kiss in the library managed to, and that would simply not do, at all—ever.

'I was about as rough and tumble as Bram is now until I was sixteen, so I very much doubt if you would have done,' she told him dourly.

'Why did you change so drastically, then?'

'My sister ran away to marry my brother's sergeant,' she said baldly. The memory of her shock and horror the night she realised Marianne was truly going to do it felt so vivid in her mind loneliness threatened all over again.

'Really?' Harry said with raised eyebrows, and for a moment she thought he was shocked a lady would want to wed a common soldier, let alone actually do it. 'I presume she succeeded. If she is half as determined as you, she will have achieved whatever she set out to,' he added, as if he admired Marianne's single-mindedness.

The very idea of him being impressed by her sister in person made a wildcat of jealousy growl possessively inside her, then flex its claws, but she backed it into a corner and threw a whole pile of blankets over it until it stopped struggling. 'Marianne is even more stubborn than I am, so of course she did. Her Daniel loved her too much to deny her anything she truly wanted, and she really and truly wanted and loved him with all her heart. I can see that now.'

'Ah, so you did not back then?' he asked, and maybe he understood her, despite her efforts to keep him at arm's length.

'No, I was still a spoilt brat,' she said with a sad shake of her head for the selfish and heedless girl she was before Marianne left home. 'Mainly spoilt by my brother and sister,' she admitted at last. 'I am four years younger than Marianne and six younger than Darius. They tolerated me following them about like an orphaned puppy, although they must have wished me at Jericho dozens of times a day. My parents were too busy to pay me much attention with a pack of boys lodged in the house to be fed and looked after as well as taught Latin and Greek.'

'No wonder you were a tomboy; you were surrounded by so many boys there was not much risk of you being anything else,' he observed with a rueful look that asked what had happened to the bold and daring Viola of her youth.

She almost wished she had an answer to his unspoken question when she looked back and wondered where all that rashness and joie de vivre had gone as well. 'Darius went away to school when he was eleven, so I relied on my sister for company when I was not sneaking out at dawn to ride racehorses for Sir Ned or refusing to learn to sew or paint watercolours or sing in Italian.'

'Who can blame you? I can do none of those things and they must have bored an enterprising girl witless. By the time you were sixteen, I suppose your sister was twenty, though, and your reckless adventures must have become harder and harder for you to get away with.'

Confound the man, she almost wished he was a

straightforward rake who would not look too hard at her youthful dilemmas while she was trying to explain why she should not hurt her brother or sister again. 'I have already told you my mother pushed me at every gentleman who crossed our path after my sister left. I blamed Marianne and, as she and Darius were hundreds of miles away by then, I felt betrayed and deserted and was not kind to either of them.'

'How did you manage it, then?' he asked sceptically. 'They were with the army, I presume posted to Portugal or Spain and well out of your reach.'

'I refused to reply to any of their letters. Marianne sent me such funny, wry and forgiving ones it was almost as if she was in the room with me. I would look up from reading them and realise how far away she really was and, even if she was back in England and camped in the next town with her husband and Darius, my mother would not have allowed us to meet. She thought I would meet a corporal I might feel like running away with or some such nonsense, I suppose.'

'I am sure there are some very fine corporals in the British Army,' Harry said lightly.

Did that mean he would quite happily see her wed one? Probably, she decided gloomily. 'No doubt, but I did not want to marry one.'

'Just as well since the world would have lost an excellent teacher if you had. Even Lucy is learning more than either of us dreamed possible, and I suspect that proves you would have been wasted on your corporal or one of those boring country gentlemen.'

'She is clever enough. She just lacks application, and I never said they were boring.'

'If they were not, you would probably have married one of them.'

'Maybe,' she almost agreed with him, and it was true that none of them had ever cost her a missed heartbeat or a single regret. 'And Lucy might surprise us all and learn to love her lessons.'

'It will certainly amaze me if she ever becomes a true scholar.'

Viola could not argue since it would astonish her, but Lucy's thirst for knowledge, or lack of it, was not what they had started out discussing, and Viola still wanted to go to her brother's wedding. 'I have not made much effort to make things up with my siblings since they came home,' she said. 'My father had retired to Bath by the time my sister came home after her Daniel was killed. Her grief felt so raw she did not even seem like my sister, and I could not help her, so I was irritable and hard-hearted and unsisterly.

'Then I chose to live in at Miss Thibett's school rather than share a room with her. I could have endured our cramped quarters and my sister crying even in her sleep, but the truth is I did not want to. I turned my back on her when she needed me, and I am so ashamed of myself, Harry. If not for my brother coming into his unexpected inheritance and inviting her to Owlet Manor to keep house for him, Marianne would still be there, and I am even more of a coward because I saw your offer of employment as a way of avoiding them all.'

'What good is you wearing a hair shirt going to do them, though?' he asked, and trust him to see through her tears and bewilderment to the heart of the matter.

'At least I can tell Marianne she is strong and brave and important to me and I love her and thank Darius for caring about me, despite everything I did to make him stop. Oh, I don't know what I can do to put things right, but I do know I have to try. I owe them a great debt of love and wish I had been there when they needed me to be. I am beginning to see how ridiculous it is, though, and you are quite right— it is impossible.' She finally admitted defeat. 'If only I had thought harder about the days and weeks passing, I could have left on the stage this morning and been nearly at Owlet Manor by now.'

'Maybe it can still be done.'

'You will lend Dulcimer to me, then? I promise to take the greatest care of her and not overface her, but there is no other way for me to get to Broadley in time for the wedding.'

'No, not Dulcimer; she was bred for speed and lacks staying power for a long ride, and your family would never let you come back here if I was to send you off alone on a nervy filly. Even you could not ride astride for forty-odd miles and stand up straight at the other end of it, Miss Yelverton.'

Oh, dear, he was calling her that and she had just let the unadorned version of his name out as if they were family or dear friends or even more intimate than that, and they definitely were not. 'Then I cannot go since the stage cannot get me there in time.'

'I shall drive you.'

'You would drive *me*, all the way to Hereford-shire?' she said slowly, feeling as if she ought not to believe her ears. Sir Harry Marbeck, the famous whip as well as a dashing gentleman who could drive the fairest in the land, offering to take her up beside him all the way to Owlet Manor for a country wedding? It sounded like an impossible idea, so she must have forced him into making a gallant offer he should not have to honour. 'Why?'

'Because you believe you need to be there and I value your care and dedication to my wards and your patience with my aunt. And because the last year and a half has taught me a great deal about family I did not think I needed to know before my cousin and his wife died. We must mend our fences when we can, Miss Yelverton, because one day it will be too late.'

'Not for you,' she protested. 'You loved your cousin and everybody here knew it.'

'How do you know?'

'Because they told me so—your aunt and your neighbours and the servants; even the doctor said you and your cousin were more like brothers than cousins and who else would he trust his children to but you?' She did not add the little man's opinion Sir Harry had come through the tragedy of losing his cousin a stronger and better man. Best not tell him how much he was loved and admired; he would not believe her and be defensive about it, as if she was accusing him of something terrible.

'Can you be ready very early tomorrow?' he said,

as if he wanted a change of subject. 'My team are well matched and good stayers, but I would rather not push them too hard. It is twenty-five miles from here to Worcester and another twenty to Broadley after that, so we will need to set out at dawn if we are to get there in time. Is this Owlet Manor of your brother's far from the town?'

'Five miles further on and definitely not as the crow flies, according to my sister, who says it is a very winding road and in no hurry to get anywhere very fast.'

'Hmm, we will need to set out well before dawn to be sure of getting there in time, then. You will need some time to bathe and dress in your finery when we get there since you will be covered in dust after all those miles of going at such speed.'

'No, this is not right; you cannot do this, Sir Harry. It is asking too much of you and your team. I should never have let you know how much I want to be there,' Viola said, shaking her head as she realised this journey would entail a gruelling drive in difficult conditions. It was simply not something a governess could expect of her employer.

'And have you pining for your family like patience on a monument all day tomorrow, Miss Yelverton? Shame on you for being such a faint heart, and my Welsh greys have been eating their heads off for far too long. It will be a nice little outing for them and a chance for me to prove their paces.'

'Truly?' she said, doubting it very much and realising how kind he was at heart to take so much trouble for an employee.

'You know I enjoy a challenge and at least you have set me one I can take up without incurring Aunt Tam's wrath. She might even tell me I am her favourite nephew if I manage to look noble enough about the sacrifice I am about to make.'

'Not when she realises she will be left in charge of the children until we return,' Viola qualified, but her heart was singing at the very idea of such an adventure with him, followed by Darius's wedding and hopefully making up with her sister as well.

'Nonsense. She will enjoy herself immensely. I will go and consult my head groom and be sure my rig is ready for the off before dawn while you break the glad news to Aunt Tam that she will be in charge of our three little rogues all day tomorrow and that they might as well all stay here until I get back so she can be queen of the castle as well. She will be delighted.'

'Hmm, I doubt it, but if your staff agree to watch Bram and Lucy like hawks as well, she will probably weather it as best she can.'

'Weather it? She will love it,' Harry argued and turned out to know his aunt a lot better than Viola did when she responded to the idea like an old warhorse scenting battle and scorned the notion she might already be tired from overseeing Bram's well-being alone for a whole week.

Chapter Twelve

'Practical enough, but you will need this,' Harry said after he eyed Miss Yelverton through the gloom and wondered how she managed to look beautiful under so much iron grey it would be hard for anyone else to pick her out from the shadows.

'Thank you,' she said warily, taking a dubious look at the robust silk scarf he was holding out to her as if she thought it might bite her.

'To keep the dust at bay; that flimsy thing will not serve once we are going at full stretch,' he told her and just caught sight of his tiger nodding sagely from his lofty perch, then hunkering into his own muffler even if he was above the worst of the dust the wheels and the horses' hooves were about to kick up.

'Oh, then I must thank you for it,' she said with a dubious look at the grey scarf he had handed her before shrugging her shoulders and undoing her fine one so she could tie his over her mouth and nose.

'Now we all look like highwaymen,' he said

lightly, and at least they could still talk through the barrier. Why did her eyes look even more unique and astonishing over the top of a muffler that ought to make her a complete quiz to match her iron-grey gown and that steely old pelisse? And as for the bonnet she was now fitting back over her enveloping cap and tightly bound hair and that makeshift mask—he wondered it had the cheek to call itself a hat at all. When he compared it to the frivolous bits of nothing he always seemed to have been buying for his ex-mistress at great expense, that monstrosity looked as if it had escaped the bonfire for far too long.

He forced his gaze away from her and on to the road just visible in the gloom of pre-dawn. He took the exit by the lodge. Then they were out on the King's Highway with two of his best grooms falling in behind to act as outriders and hopefully make their dash for Owlet Manor look more respectable to her waiting family.

Miss Yelverton sat stiffly against his side at first, as if she thought he might have something catching if she got too close, but acting like a machine-driven governess in an open carriage that would have to go as fast as this one would as soon as it was light enough would be dangerous. He let the curricle swing wider than strictly necessary at the first bend in their way so she had to grab the side of the carriage to stay safe.

At last he felt her relax and let her lithe body sway with the motion of his curricle and felt a bit guilty for deliberately making her shift fluidly with their

motion, as he knew very well she could after that
dash across his park on Dulcimer what seemed like
months ago rather than barely two weeks. He was a
bad man, but the feel of her body moving with the
curves of the road when she was this close to him in
such a tight space was intimate and seductive and a
suitable punishment for a frustrated man who ought
to know better.

To distract himself, he added up the miles they
must travel to get her to this wedding with time for
her to bathe and dress in something less grey and
practical. Forty-five to Broadley and five more and a
few extra to allow for those crows that kept on flying
in straight lines. His horses could do sixteen miles an
hour on a clear road in full racing mode, but he could
not expect a lady to mould her every movement to
the vehicle all the way there, or cheer him along as a
friend might if they were doing this for fun.

He did not want to change horses too often, so
maybe he could even manage to nurse his team all
the way there if he was not too hard on them. His
best rate of travel could be not much more than ten
miles an hour, then. That would allow for traffic and
toll gates and the occasional farm cart getting in the
way. After four to five hours of sitting next to Miss
Yelverton, he would run mad or be a candidate for
sainthood.

'Have you ever travelled this way before?' he
asked to distract himself from his saintly ordeal. As
far as he could see, there was a thin line between

sainthood and madness—perhaps he would be both at the same time.

'No. We lived in Dorset when I was a child and, apart from going to Kent to see Darius after his training at Shorncliffe Camp, and the odd visit to my grandparents in Devon as a child, this is as far as I ever travelled from home.'

Goodness, he now knew more about Miss Yelverton's former life than he had managed to find out in the last eighteen months. 'You are a real south-country girl, then. How come you and your family did not visit whoever left your brother his manor house so unexpectedly, or did the man who bequeathed it to him insist on only meeting the males of the family?'

'No. My mother's Uncle Hubert was a very determined recluse. I believe he told my grandparents they should take their chattering rattlepate of a child away and never come back when they took Mama to visit him as a small child. He threatened not to leave his brother a penny piece of his money or a square inch of land if he ever came back, unless he did it alone. I am delighted to say my grandfather refused to go to Owlet Manor without his wife or daughter, so they had no contact at all for the rest of their lives. We had no idea Great-Uncle Hubert would leave all he had to Darius when he died. Indeed, we three did not even know we had a great-uncle until he left my brother everything as a reward for not bothering him as a child or man and for fighting for his country all those years. I suppose that means he kept an eye on his brother's family from afar. How else could he have known Darius is a brave man and not one of the go-on-then officers my sister told me about in her letters?'

'Would that all those who are so brave could be similarly rewarded,' Harry said, thinking about the terrible cost of some of that service and counting his own blessings as he frowned at the road ahead.

'Indeed, my sister had to petition for mere shillings from the army after Daniel died, and she had family willing to help her. I have no idea how soldiers dismissed from the service feed their families on little or nothing a week.'

'How indeed?' Harry said gloomily and resolved to double his contribution to the charities for old and injured soldiers he already supported. 'Has Aunt Tam told you the love of her life was killed fighting in the American Wars? Now we are over there fighting another, I think she feels the waste of young lives more than ever, and it makes her even more irritable.'

'Thank you for telling me. It explains a great deal.'

'Goodness knows there is much about her to explain,' he said because he knew she was being polite about his dragon aunt.

'We manage to rub along together tolerably well most of the time,' Miss Yelverton said, as if she was still very conscious Aunt Tam was family and she was only an employee. Not that he thought of her as an *only* anyone, but confound the woman, why did she always have to be so correct and precise and put their distinctions of rank and fortune in front of him all the time? When she was not being wild and commanding and infinitely kissable, of course, just as she was the day Bram fell in the lake and when she was in joint charge of Lucy and Emma's sickroom with him.

He let his mind linger fondly on a memory of her not caring who saw her shapely legs as she rode astride his prized filly like a warrior queen at the head of an army. With so much of her company still to get through today, he dared not even think about that stolen kiss in the library. So he lingered on the delightful fantasy of doing it again as soon as he could for a few silent moments and hastily reminded himself to keep his attention on his horses before he overturned them like a rank amateur.

Knowing about the complicated and contrary woman under all the Miss Yelverton disguises made it feel all the more frustrating she was hiding behind her governess barriers again. Knowing there was a very different woman behind them longing to be let out felt like a delicious secret only he knew about.

It was just as well he had to concentrate on his team and the kinks in the road that could trip up an unwary driver, so the first few hours of their journey flew by without too much trouble. At last they were as far on as Worcester and it was still not even nine o'clock. With good luck and no heavy wagons in the way, they should be in time for Darius Yelverton's wedding.

Odd how he knew her brother's first name, but not Miss Yelverton's. He smiled at the notion of a complete stranger eyeing him with even more suspicion as he greeted the man so familiarly that he must remember not to do so. Even more odd how he felt some of the tension leave Miss Yelverton's body as they forged on through the old city and out across the New Bridge, after he had had a brief debate with his head groom about the state of the horses and whether they needed a change. Then they were out the other side and on the road to Herefordshire. Luckily Culworth agreed the team and the riding horses were all in good order and not too hot, so another twenty miles would probably not do them any harm.

'We are over halfway there,' he said encouragingly to his passenger.

'I can never thank you enough for doing this for me and my family, Sir Harry,' she said, as if that gratitude was a burden she would rather not carry, stiff-necked female that she was.

'Please do not mention it,' he replied. 'No, really, you must not thank me again. I am delighted to help and give my team a good run at the same time. Stop being embarrassed about having to accept my help, Miss Yelverton; it is mortifying for both of us and I am sure you would not want me to be mortified.'

'I might,' she said, and he could tell she was smiling even without being able to see her mouth.

There was warmth and something a lot more tempting in her clear blue gaze as she met his briefly, then looked away. It broke one of his chains, that almost intimate, half-conspiratorial look from the real Miss Yelverton under the governess clothes and *pretend I am not here* manner. He let himself wonder facetiously if she had a silky version of her usual armour in the small valise she handed to his tiger to be strapped on to the back with Harry's own better clothes and a change of linen for his journey home. Even the thought of her dressed in fine silk or satin that would love her body whether she wanted it to or not was a fantasy too far for a man who must sit this close to her for another twenty miles or more before he could turn back without her.

'Consider it done, then,' he murmured so softly not even the tiger perched behind them could hear him for the noise of the wheels and the horses.

Now she looked flustered and he was half-sorry for it, but she must learn not to play with fire. They still had almost six months left on their ridiculous contract, so she was still a lady more or less living under his roof and definitely under his protection in the most protective sense of the word. *Saint Harry the Martyr*, he mocked himself silently. What would he be like at the end of another six months? From here it looked like the stuff of nightmares and somehow he had to keep thinking of her as stiff and steely Miss Yelverton, not the fearless amazon she was that day at the lake, or the kind and caring woman who helped him nurse Lucy and Emma when his terror for their survival felt sharp as a knife in the heart.

'Marianne! Oh, it's so good to see you again,' Miss Yelverton shouted out even before Harry halted his team outside the farmyard door to the venerable

old manor house as her sister had come running out
to see who this strange vehicle belonged to.

'I could hardly believe my eyes, Viola,' the taller
and even more slender Yelverton sister replied, looking as if she was about to cry. Harry was almost glad
he was still perched up here with a team to hold together so he could be stalwartly male about the sisters' joy at being reunited. He supposed he ought to
be awed by the speed at which his Viola scrambled
down from her lofty perch, but as the tired team still
managed to object to her hasty departure, he managed to click his tongue impatiently instead. *Hmm,
Viola*—now, wasn't that an unexpected and roman-
tic sort of a name for his own particular governess?
Did it suit her? Yes, he decided, and managed to tear
his gaze from her with her muffler hastily unwound
and the joy on her dust-marred face fully revealed.
He was in a bad way if she still looked exceptional
with all that dirt making her a mud-coloured lady instead of a steely grey one. Even her gown was over-
laid with streaks of road dust where the folds were
open to the rushing air of their swift progress from
the Cotswolds.

'Good grief, Stratford—what the devil are you
doing here?' Harry demanded as his Viola hugged
her sister again and he focused his attention on the
tall man standing behind Marianne Whoever-she-
was-now.

'I could ask you the same question if I was rude
enough to come out with it, Marbeck,' Viscount
Stratford told him genially and tried to look as if he

dropped in for a country wedding most weeks when he could find one.

'It was the only way to get Miss Yelverton here in time,' Harry replied, as if that explained everything, and, if Viola was to have enough time to get herself bathed and groomed and suitably transformed in time for her brother's wedding, it would have to do for now.

'My niece,' Stratford explained not very informatively as a dark-haired girl peeped around the corner of the door into the house and looked as if she dearly wished she had not.

'Miss Defford,' Harry said with as gallant a bow as he could manage from up here.

'Sir,' she whispered and, after another terrified look, turned tail and scurried back the way she had come. Harry vaguely recalled someone writing to him that the Defford girl was far too shy and quiet to take when she made her come out this spring, and here was proof they were quite right.

'You must be Sir Harry Marbeck,' a much sterner and more sceptical-looking stranger informed him with a hard look Harry could imagine him using on raw recruits when he found them sadly wanting. 'I am Darius Yelverton,' the stiff-backed former soldier told him, as if he had a rifle and an officer's sword close by that he always kept handy for occasions like this, and never mind if it was his wedding day—he still knew where to find them.

'A pleasure to meet you, Mr Yelverton,' Harry made himself lie with a smile barely on the right side of polite. The man was Viola's brother, after all, and the man was about to get married, so they could hardly brawl or call one another out because the man's sister was governess to his wards and Yelverton did not trust bad Sir Harry Marbeck to keep his hands off her.

'Oh, for goodness' sake, Darius,' Viola intervened, rolling her eyes towards the heavens as she took in her brother's stiff posture and challenging gaze. 'When will you realise I am a grown woman and quite capable of fighting my own battles, if and when they need fighting?'

'When hell freezes over, little Sister,' the man said, but he huffed a great sigh and met Harry's rueful look over his sister's head with one of his own. 'Thank you for bringing her here,' Yelverton said, as if he was trying very hard to mean it while wondering what was wrong with the stage.

His smile for his sister was genuine and affectionate, though, and Harry was glad he had driven all this way to reunite the siblings on this special day, but he did not think he would feel welcome in Yelverton's stable yard while his horses were being rubbed down, rested, then watered, ready for their journey back to Broadley and an inn where they could be left when a new team had been hired for Harry's home run.

'My pleasure,' he said truly enough because it was pleasing to see Viola so happy with her brother and sister. 'If you could direct me to your stable yard, I would like these beasts to have a short rest before we go back again.'

'Even I am not such a yahoo as all that, Sir Harry. Now you are here, you must stay to see me married and give your horses a proper rest. My sisters are sure to insist on it, even if my future wife cannot leave her room and add her voice to the mix. Apparently I am not supposed to see her until she walks down the aisle.' Again there was that hint of warning behind the man's bland words, as if he wanted a chance to assess Harry's suitability as an employer of attractive young women and never mind polite invitations to his wedding for a complete stranger.

'Yes, we do insist,' Marianne put in with a delightful smile that told Harry exactly why Stratford was dogging her footsteps like a possessive guard dog.

The lady was taller and more openly warm-hearted than her sister, and what a potent contrast that smile of hers was to Viola's more guarded one. This was how *his* Yelverton sister might have been if she was the one who fell in love with a good man all those years ago. He recognised so many similarities in the way they stood and spoke and braved the world, and so many differences he would be able to tell them apart in the pitch-dark, just as he was sure Stratford could.

Seeing another fool in a similar state of guarded frustration to his own made him see how far gone he was in fascination with a woman he could not have. He wanted Viola more than ever now he knew her name and had seen the full promise and potential in her steady blue gaze as she looked back at him from the safety of her sister's side, as if she had been reunited with a part of herself as well as a much-loved sister. He knew so much more about her now, as she stood there with her sister's arm about her waist and a smile like sunshine breaking out on a cloudy day on her grubby face. So it was not just want, then, was it? He was horribly certain all of a sudden it was far more than a physical itch for a furtively attractive young woman. Viola Yelverton could turn his whole world upside down if he let her, and he was perilously close to doing just that.

Chapter Thirteen

'Sir Harry is extremely handsome,' Marianne said meaningfully as she gently soaped Viola's hair. Even after all the brushing they had given it before Viola got in the tub, it was shedding dust into the bathwater along with all the suds it took to wash the rest off her person after her hasty journey.

'Umm,' Viola managed to murmur through her mostly closed lips as she screwed her eyes shut and was relieved when her sister poured clean water over her head from the next jug in line. Just as well she could hardly say much at the moment since there was so little she wanted to say about Harry Marbeck to her much-too-interested sister. He was very handsome indeed. There was no getting away from the bare facts of the matter. Yet his looks were only the start of his unique charm; now she knew him so much better, his surface attractions were not even half of his potent appeal.

'And dashing,' Marianne continued relentlessly.

'Hmm,' Viola agreed, because he was.

'And it was considerate and kind of him to bring you here so fast if there truly was no other way for you to get here in time for Darius and Fliss's wedding.'

'Hmm, hmm.'

'Oh, for goodness' sake, I have done rinsing your hair now, Viola, so stop pretending you cannot talk,' Marianne said, as if it was annoying of her not to parry all that bare fact with a hot denial or two.

'If you want me to hold a rational conversation on irrational matters, you should wait until you are not trying to drown me at the same time.'

'You and your rational conversations,' Marianne said, as if she thought Viola was being deliberately obstructive, and that was fair enough, because she was.

'And you and your irrational questions,' Viola parried, rubbing her already wildly curling hair with a towel and eyeing her sister warily.

'We have not changed very much, have we?'

'I have; I am ready to admit I was wrong all those years ago and stayed angry with you and Darius for leaving me to be Mama's last chick in the nest for far too long. I am truly sorry for it now, Marianne.'

Marianne looked uncomfortable at that admission and now it was her turn to avoid the subject with the practicalities by helping Viola comb out the wild tangles in her blonde hair and clucking over the bird's nest Viola's would have made out of it if she was not here to patiently intervene. 'You always

were too impatient with it,' she scolded and play-
fully slapped Viola's hand away so she could tease
out the knots herself.

For a while they were silent as Marianne concentrated on her task and Viola made herself sit still and
enjoy being clean again as well as revelling in being
gently fussed over by her big sister. 'You have made
this room lovely, Marianne,' Viola said as she sat in
the autumn sunlight with her sister brushing her long
curls into neatness, the warmth of the September sun
beginning to dry the heavy mass, so it should not be
too long before it could be hastily dressed for a wedding and never mind if parts of it would still be damp
for the ceremony and beyond.

It would curl wildly, so no chance of her looking
like a proper governess today, but why would she
want to on a day when Darius was about to marry a
woman who made him look boyish and carefree and
besotted whenever he thought about her and even her
darling elder sister was clearly on the edge of falling in love again?

'I did it for you,' Marianne said simply, and there
it was, all the warmth and love Viola had done her
best to shut out of her life for the last seven years,
fool that she was.

'Thank you,' Viola managed to say and blinked
several times to stem a rush of tears that threatened
to change her into someone a lot more open and vulnerable than she wanted to be in front of Harry and
at exactly the wrong moment as well. 'I must not cry,
Nan, not now.'

'True, neither of us ought to turn up at the chapel with piggy eyes and tear-streaked faces, although I am not sure I can keep such self-control in place all the way through the wedding. I am so happy Darius is marrying the love of his life today instead of a golden dolly. I might cry over their happiness from sheer relief he stopped being stubborn as a mule in time to convince Fliss he truly loves her and always will.'

'Was there truly a danger he would marry for money?'

'Of course there was—the great idiot was convinced he had to marry a fortune for our sakes as well as to get the money to mend and improve this poor old house and the farms.'

'Why?'

'He wanted us to live here and be ladies of leisure,' Marianne told her with a roll of her eyes to say what a ridiculous notion it was.

'At such cost to his freedom? I would rather work until I am old and grey, and I doubt we would be good at it anyway.'

'You know he is such a stubborn idiot that when he gets an idea in his head it is like chipping at stone to get it out again.'

'Yes, I do, and if you had anything to do with chiselling away at him so he would end up with this Fliss of his, then well done. He has always been as stubborn as a rock once he gets an idea in his head. This house does not look as poor as you told me it would have to be for a while when you came here, by the way. In fact, it looks as if someone has spent a great deal of money on it to get it into a fit state for them to begin their marriage in style here.'

'Yes, *someone* has,' her sister said with a disapproving frown, and her story of the last few weeks here and why that particular someone felt he wanted to spend so much money on a house that was not his took up so much time that in the end they both had to scurry to be ready in time for the wedding, since their fingers slowed as Marianne's tale grew more and more intent on certain Viscounts and their managing ways and straying relatives.

At the end of it, Viola hastily helped Marianne into the delicious azure silk-and-gauze gown their sister-in-law-to-be had ordered for her matron of honour, and Marianne laced Viola into her own best gown of figured muslin with an azure satin underskirt that Marianne had brought with her from Bath, so their mother would not be able to cut it up to make christening gowns for deserving families. After all, why would her ungrateful younger daughter need such finery in her chosen profession?

Mrs Yelverton had always disliked this gown, as Viola had fought for one with a modest neckline and subtle shades, instead of being cut a whisper away from revealing far too much of her. Even as they raced to be ready in time, Viola was relieved her mother was too preoccupied with her own toilette to come and harangue her younger daughter about her unfortunate choices in life all over again. Then she and Marianne were both ready and they stood back to examine one another for stray curls or dangling threads.

'You look even more beautiful than usual,' she told Marianne, although those tears were threatening again at the sight of her big sister looking so effortlessly and unconsciously lovely in her light and elegant gown with her hair loosely and far more flatteringly dressed than usual. She silently blessed this Fliss Grantham, soon to be Yelverton, for knowing exactly what suited Marianne and making sure she wore it on this special day. She had not even met her yet and she already knew she was going to like her.

'And you look as lovely as ever, Viola.'

For once, Viola let herself hope her sister was telling her the truth, for this was one day when she could allow herself to believe it for an hour or two. Her inner rebel wanted Harry to see her at her best for once instead of her plain and workaday worst. Fool that she was, she wanted him to be startled by the real woman under the steely disguise. 'Handsome is as handsome does,' she joked with her big sister for the first time in far too many years.

'Remember how Mama used to tell us that when she thought we were getting above ourselves. I fear neither of us pleased her much after we grew up.'

They exchanged rueful glances as they heard the flurry and fluster of their mother bustling along the corridor to pick at them about their appearance and conduct. Viola knew they were both wondering what had happened to the capable wife and mother who ran the Rectory with bustling serenity when they were little. Best not look back and blame themselves for disappointing their mother's best hopes for her daughters and remember instead they still loved one another, despite the differences time and maturity only emphasised.

Harry already knew the woman was beautiful, so it should have come as no surprise to see her as nature intended—well, not quite as bare as that—but she was much less guarded and more carefree than he had ever witnessed her being before. If that was an example of the sort of gown Miss Yelverton used to wear in the ballrooms and drawing rooms of Bath, he should have spent far more time there and less in fashionable London. It was simply elegant and several years out of date, but the clean lines, lovely colour and high waist suited her elegant figure to perfection. Of course he ought to prefer her in her gloomiest schoolmistress gown, but he still liked her better like this.

He was expert enough on female fashion to know a London modiste would sneer at the lack of wadding in the hemline to bell her gown out. The sleeves were puffs of gauze and lace and the bodice cut far too demurely to give a rake more ideas than he already had about her delightful figure and all the other things that made her uniquely herself under its silky covering. Yet her azure satin underskirt almost finished off his treasured composure as it shifted and slid around her curves.

She could not know how seductively it clung in

all the right places to make a man acutely aware of the woman underneath it because she was just not that sort of woman. If she had any idea how it could affect a man, her whole delicious ensemble would soon be cut up to make finery for Lucy or Emma, he decided with a smile that felt much too fond for comfort. He hastily looked away from the more than delightful sight of her and met Stratford's acute gaze full on instead. He shook his head to say no need to worry; he knew the lady was out of bounds and he could carry on burning for her without her knowing for another six months.

Then he stared at the distant hills for a moment to try to forget how dearly he wanted to kiss Miss Yelverton's deliciously parted lips as she did her best to pretend she was listening to whatever her mother was whispering in her ear, but somehow his gaze slewed slyly back to the feminine magnet who made the rest of the women here seem all but invisible.

There were flowers twined into her hair. Her sister must have wound them through her shining blonde curls and caught the intriguing weight of it into a cleverly sophisticated chignon instead of the usual tight bun he knew must hurt her with all the pins it would take to keep it that way now he had seen the length and thickness of it on show. It looked like a crime to confine all that life and energy into a locked-down version of itself, which was a metaphor for the woman herself, now he came to think about it. Best not do much more of that, he chided himself as he felt Stratford's gaze rest thoughtfully on him again.

Harry was glad Yelverton himself was far too taken up with his fiery-haired pocket Venus to notice how hungrily Harry wanted to gawp at his little sister, revealed in her true colours for once. Now Stratford was furtively gazing at the elder one with a dazed look of wonder in his eyes, as if he could hardly believe his luck at finding the most unlikely lady anyone could have thought of for him to long for and adore. What would their protective elder brother have to say about his sisters being secretly lusted after by two unsuitable aristocrats if he could only spare the time to worry about them right now?

Well, no—to be just, Stratford was a lot more suitable than he was, now he came to think about it. Sir Harry Marbeck was not an aristocrat in the truest sense of the word—he had no seat in the House of Lords, and if he wanted a place at the next coronation, he supposed he would have to earn it. The notion of going into the House of Commons just for the privilege of perhaps being chosen to witness fat Prinny being made into a king one day was comical enough to make him forget how much he longed for a Miss Yelverton in his bed for a whole second, so that was some good Prinny had done someone all unknowingly.

At least the little chapel a few hundred yards from the manor house was too small to cram in very many guests. Harry did not know any of them apart from Stratford, so they would not know how unlike his usual self he was today. He listened to Viola's father marry his son and daughter-in-law and learned to respect the gentle and sincere man even more than he already did for standing up for Viola when she needed him to. The Reverend Yelverton gave a short but thought-provoking sermon on the subject of love and the joint enterprise of a true and lasting marriage, with a gentle glance for his own wife to say it had been so for them, however different they were at heart.

It made Harry ponder the difference love and goodwill could make to marriage as he compared his own incompatible parents with Viola's. Her father and mother had made their life together work somehow; his parents must have been too set in their differences to even try to. It was another shift in his thinking he once thought he would never make.

He had been very resolute about not lusting after ladies who might expect him to marry them right up to the day he saw Miss Viola Yelverton shining against her will in the spring sunshine a year and a half ago. No, that was not quite right—he had been even more determined to resist that longing since he first set eyes on her. Yet perhaps her father was right and a true marriage was made up from compromise and tolerance, but if that was all it was, could it be truly happy? Harry left love off the list because he had always thought it was a myth, but Christian and Jane loved deeply and sincerely, and perhaps the apparently ill-assorted Reverend Yelverton and his matchmaking wife did so as well.

Anyway, there was no need for him to worry about such deep questions at another man's wedding. But if his smart London friends and fellow Oxford adventurers could see him enjoying a country wedding full of strangers and the once aloof and remote Viscount Stratford, they would wonder what on earth had become of his sangfroid since he left town. The Harry of a couple of years ago would agree with them, yet enjoy it he still did.

He shared a very gentle walk back to the house with Viola and her learned but breathless father. He ate fine food in a hastily cleared and whitewashed great hall and even danced a merry and vigorous dance with the new Mrs Yelverton before her husband intervened and carried her off to adore and yearn for all the way down the room and back, then around and in between the weaves of a country dance. Harry knew how Yelverton felt—well, almost, apart from the love part of their day.

He also had a desperate urge to grab Viola, for she really was Viola without her Miss Yelverton armour on, and dance her around the room and outside into the recently tamed garden. Out there he was sure there would be privacy enough to seduce her with hot kisses and hasty promises his inner cynic knew could only lead to another country wedding. And how could he allow that disaster when he had sworn off marriage practically in his cradle?

'It is high time I left,' he said abruptly when he finally managed to weave his solitary way across the room and interrupt some buffoon who was attempting to flirt with Viola. The man was lucky he did not get a fist planted sharply in his overly comfortable midriff, Harry decided savagely, and managed to cool his glare enough to give the encroaching fellow a haughty look instead of an open challenge to eat grass before breakfast.

'I will go and change,' she said with a regretful look for her brother and sister, and of course she hated the idea of leaving so soon.

'No, you must stay with your family for a few days as we discussed on the way here. Aunt Tam and I can cope with my brats between us and you have a good many half-days' leave untaken to catch up with, Miss Yelverton. Please do not argue and claim you have no right to take a short holiday with your family now we have got you here. I am ready for the children's starts now and the nursery maid promised never to flirt with the under-gardener when she is supposed to be on duty again, so she can help me keep them out of mischief until you are back.'

'She is lucky you agreed to keep her on after that flirtation nearly cost Bram his life,' Miss Yelverton told him, and he regretted her return, then eyed the lovely Viola in front of him and decided that difference was never going to work on him again.

'If her sweetheart had not dived into the lake and fished Bram out in time to save his life, she might have lost her place, but he did and saved Bram and her job. We have agreed to say no more about it as long as Carrie puts all her energy into watching those two little demons like a hawk from now on.'

'Even if you feel you can trust her, I am not sure I do,' Viola murmured darkly and made another chip at his composure. She truly cared about his family. Suddenly he had a rosy image of all three children and himself and Viola melded into a new one; a heady little universe of love and support and humour where they could raise his cousin's children together with their own.

Remember your mother leaving you as if she was going to a party and absent-mindedly decided not to come home again at the end of it, Marbeck, he ordered himself austerely. There had not been much love, support or humour in his immediate family when he was growing up, so how could he believe in it now?

'Whatever Carrie is asked to do from now on, you can trust me to hold her to her promise. I will be even more furious with you if you turn up at Chantry Old Hall before Monday than I was with her after I realised exactly why Bram had enough freedom to make his way on to the roof of the boathouse before falling off it in such spectacular style.'

She eyed him thoughtfully, as if trying to judge whether he truly meant it. 'Very well,' she agreed at last and gave him a half-smile and a shrug as she glanced at her family again and relaxed her Miss Yelverton pose. 'Thank you,' she said, gave him her best Viola smile and threatened a powerful wanting he dare not put into words even in his own head. 'I would love to spend a couple of days with them all,' she admitted. 'And by Monday I will be just as glad to return to real life,' she added with a rueful shrug.

'Until Monday, then,' he said with an inane smile and a silent curse. He had flirted with foreign princesses and picky society beauties, exchanged heady looks and meaningful smiles with the cream of the demi-monde and been entertained and intrigued by the promise and secrets in hungry feminine eyes ever since he dared think of himself as a man. Now he could not even hang on to his composure to bid his wards' governess a gracious farewell.

Chapter Fourteen

Viola stepped off the Worcester to Bath stage less than halfway to its destination and breathed a sigh of relief. She had missed the honeyed stone and generous curves of the Cotswold Hills over the four whole days she had been away and it felt as if she was almost home. Now all she had to do was hire the battered old gig and equally battered old driver from the inn. Once they were safely in Marbeck Magna, someone would be willing to take a message up to the Hall so Harry would send a carriage for her. The ancient vehicle was too old to go all the way up to Garrard House, but at least once she was in the village she would be nearly there.

Except Harry saved her the trouble by taking a great deal more of it himself than an employer ought to over the return of his wards' governess. Here he was, driving in through the inn yard in his everyday curricle, very different to the one they raced to Herefordshire in, and her heart did a silly little dance as she realised he had come to meet her.

'Emma, Sir Harry,' she greeted them with a smile that felt much too wide to hide her delight at the very sight of the man. 'I hope you have not driven all this way solely for my sake.'

'We wanted to surprise you and get away from the children for an hour, Miss Yelverton. They have been driving me mad all day, but Uncle Harry said there was only room for one of us and I am the only one who deserves a treat. I am to sit in the middle and we hope you do not mind being squashed up a bit, but it was too nice a day to bring the chaise.'

'You are not exactly large, Emma, and of course I do not,' Viola told her with another delighted smile.

She was seeing Harry again even sooner than she'd expected to, and this was what happened when she did not have a long, slow drive to his home village to give her time to prepare for the sight of him looking even more handsome and dashing than she remembered across that gap of trivial-sounding days. Thank goodness for Emma's slight body between them, then. Her presence ought to put aside Viola's yearning for Harry to have missed her even half as much as she had him.

'Have they been very naughty?' she asked as she hopped into the light carriage with the help of a passing groom. Very soon they were out of the yard and back on the open road. It was hard not to admire Harry's skill as a whip or his lithe and manly form as he kept his spirited team to an easy pace.

'They were very good for the whole day Uncle Harry was gone. I was really worried,' Emma answered for him, and Viola only just managed not to laugh out loud at her earnest expression. Harry avoided her eyes, but his shoulders shook a little as he stared at the road ahead.

'What happened then?' Viola managed to say solemnly.

'When Uncle Harry came home they went back to normal.'

'Imagine my relief,' Harry said blandly.

Again Viola felt the tug of humour pull them closer—drat it, she did not want to feel any closer to the man than she already did. Well, that was not quite true; she did want to be closer to him. Very close indeed, if the terrible truth be known, but it was far better not. 'I am,' she replied with a rueful smile at those hills she had wanted to see so badly. It was probably him she had been yearning for as if a vital part of her had gone missing, but as it felt impossible to go back to being stern and aloof Miss Yelverton in his presence, she could not afford to be too honest with herself now.

The rest of September rolled on and autumn began to tint the first of the leaves so there was a mellow quality to the long slant of the sunlight now. Viola thought the younger two children might be a bit quieter and more willing to learn than they were before that dreadful fortnight when all three faced danger, but that was wishful thinking. One afternoon when she was almost daring to believe Lucy had settled down, she realised the little girl had stolen out of the schoolroom while Viola was too busy with Bram's Latin vocabulary to notice.

'That is very good and please carry on, Bram. Emma can test you while I find out where your little sister has sneaked off to while we were busy, and please do not forget she will be in serious trouble for this, will you?' Viola warned him in case he decided he had been good for long enough as well.

After a hasty look in the day nursery and a quick word with Carrie the nursery maid, they decided the little madam must have stolen downstairs to rout about in the empty bedrooms. Following her at the double, Viola shouted Lucy's name and never mind if truly polite ladies never raised their voices. There was a muffled crash followed by heavy silence. Lucy must have decided there was no point trying to hide after that and appeared on the landing outside one of the best spare bedchambers, still doing her best to pretend the noise was nothing to do with her.

'And what have you been up to this time, young lady?' Viola said with a deep sigh to say she was nearly at the end of her tether.

'It wasn't me.'

'Who else could it have been, Lucy? Now you are adding lying to whatever sins you have been committing and you know perfectly well it was naughty to slip away and wander about the house looking for trouble like this.'

'I don't like fractions.'

'Who does? Now you had best tell me what you have done straight away and get it out of the way, before I think up some really fiendish ones to punish you for whatever disaster you just caused.'

'I dropped the box,' Lucy mumbled sulkily.

'Which box?'

'The Corinna lady's one.'

Who on earth did she mean? Ah, of course, Miss Marbeck had told her Harry's mother was called Corinna. 'Show me,' she said sternly.

Lucy led her into an unused bedchamber and pointed at the once beautiful marquetry writing slope lying upended on the floor.

'Oh, Lucy, how could you be so careless?' Viola scolded as she took in the damage.

'I didn't mean to.'

'No, you never do.'

So of course Lucy cried and Viola felt guilty and tried not to show it. 'You will have to apologise to Sir Harry,' she told Lucy, but of course that was not a particularly fearsome punishment, and Lucy began to look almost cheerful again. 'And you must pay for the damage out of your pin money.'

'That's not fair. It will cost more than I've got.'

'You should have thought of that before you meddled, Lucy, and I have no sympathy with you, so you can stop pretending to cry. Ah, here is Carrie come from looking everywhere else in the house except here, which is the last place you ought to be, by the way, Lucy Marbeck. Please take Miss Lucy to the nursery and see she stops there for an hour or so with nothing to do, Carrie. I will pick this poor box up as best I can and inform Miss Marbeck that it has been damaged.'

From the look Carrie gave her, she thought Viola had the worst task ahead of her, and she was probably right. Sighing for the damage to the fine mahogany box when it opened on landing, Viola retrieved a cut-glass inkwell from where it had rolled into the far corner of the room. Thank goodness it was empty and had landed on the fine Turkish rug, so it looked undamaged. She gathered up the sand box and some sticks of sealing wax, then very gently did her best to turn the box upright without doing yet more damage. She heard a mechanism click and nearly fumbled the box herself when a hidden spring shot out a secret drawer. Taking a more secure hold on the box and its unexpected contents, she gathered it up and put it on the bed so she could see what was damage and what had been designed to come apart.

There were two slender drawers anyone not aware they existed would be hard pushed to guess lay under the neat partitions for the finest materials a letter writer might need. Inside them were three little books, some letters and a fine leather pouch. Unable to resist her own curiosity now and feeling guilty after punishing Lucy for hers, she emptied the pouch into her hands and plumped down on the bed, holding two valuable rings in her hand. Viola could see that one was a wide gold wedding band. The other was a rather heavy and old-fashioned circlet set with diamonds and emeralds. She heard something crackle inside the pouch and delved into it and fetched out a tiny slip of paper. It read *my fetters*, and the words were written with such force the pen had spluttered and left a blot at the end.

Viola put her hand to her mouth and realised they must be Harry's mother's wedding and betrothal rings, so she should pack it all back up and hand it to him. Except he would consign it to a dark attic and forget Lucy ever dropped it and showed Viola the box's secret by accident. She could not resist a look inside the neat books, and once she started reading, she forgot to feel guilty. The writing was so tiny she had to hold it close to read it. At first the puzzle of reading the words the lady must have written secretively and with a silver pencil so she could hide it in this cunning box caught her interest. Then the words caught her imagination and she read on, fascinated by the sad little tale they revealed.

Chapter Fifteen

'Miss Yelverton, what on earth are you doing up here at this time of night?' Harry demanded after he managed to get his jumping nerves and his thundering libido under some sort of control.

'Hush!' Viola ordered, as if he was being tiresome, and slipped through the outside door of the library, then closed it after her. She looked as if she had far more important things on her mind than propriety and the mile walk all the way up here with only a quarter-moon's worth of light to guide her. 'You must read these,' she told him and looked urgent and agitated about whatever they were.

He frowned and refused to take the small silk-bound books she was holding out to him. 'Why did you risk coming all the way here so late at night, Viola?' he asked and expected her to poker up and remember who they were at the sound of her first name on his lips. Perhaps then she would turn around and storm off as hastily as she came here, from the windswept and deliciously ruffled look of her as she stood there like a fantasy he ought not to be having about a lady.

'I had to wait until your aunt was safely in bed and she took for ever to admit she was tired tonight.'

'Aye, she is stubborn as a mule about such things when she is not pretending to be a frail old lady, but you should still not be here.' *And you never spoke truer, Marbeck,* he told himself as need to get her even more windswept and ruffled and wanting him back as desperately as he wanted her stormed through him like a January gale.

'You must read these and the letters I found with them,' she told him, and he wondered what she would do if he simply fell on her and begged.

'Why?' he asked distractedly.

'Your mother wrote them,' she said, and a slap in the face would have felt better. His inner demons subsided in the face of that cold reality and he stared at the slim books and a bundle of letters in her hand as if he found it hard to understand what they were.

'That sounds like a very good reason why I should not, then,' he replied sharply and turned his back on her to keep those demons locked up long enough to get her to go away. Now the shock of her words was wearing off, he did not want to see her flush with annoyance, then set her delightful mouth in her determination to make him listen to her. Bad enough he knew that was how she would react to his 'no', let alone seeing it happen.

'No, you have to look. These prove that she was

not how you think she was. She had to do something drastic in order to save herself and you.'

'And where did you find this fairy story?' he said harshly.

'Inside her writing box,' she said almost guiltily, as if she knew he would not want her to know anything about his dear departed mama, but had read them anyway.

'My father ordered it to be burnt,' he argued, recalling the day a couple of years after his mother left them when his father's cold fury turned hot and he raged through the house, looking for his wife's favourite belongings to destroy.

'Apparently an elderly servant rescued it and took it home, then gave it to your aunt when she came to live at Garrard House. Miss Marbeck was too worried about the children at the time to take much notice and put it in an unused bedroom and forgot about it until today when Lucy found it and dropped it. Apparently the woman was afraid she would be accused of stealing it if she kept it, since it carries the Marbeck crest, and in the end, your aunt thought she was very glad to get it off her hands.'

'But Aunt Tam kept it anyway?'

'Why not? It is beautifully made and fitted out, and one day Lucy or Emma might like to have it and make use of it.'

'Then why is it not still sitting there forgotten and waiting for that far-off day when they need such an elaborate writing box?' he asked abruptly. He had put his mother in a special limbo for neglectful parents years ago and did not want her to be let out of it and manipulating Viola's soft heart.

'The secret mechanism flew open when Lucy dropped the box,' she explained and looked as if she still thought he needed to know what his mother had said, and he definitely did not.

'She has read these things, then?' he barked as fury roared through him at the thought of his mother's selfish outpourings sullying Lucy's innocence, even all these years after the woman left to meet her lover.

'No. When she dropped the box, the crash gave her away. She had sneaked out of the schoolroom and must have heard me calling her and panicked, so it slid out of her hands. It is too heavy for her to carry far, so goodness knows what she thought she was going to do with it anyway. Carry it off to her lair and pick through it later, I suppose,' Viola said, and she seemed oblivious to the emotions he was trying so hard to keep inside as she stood there describing Lucy's misdeeds when hers felt so much worse.

'She did not read anything, then?'

'No, but I have. You have no idea of the real story behind your parents' marriage, Harry. He fell head over heels in love with her—your father was so passionately in love and insistent he must marry her she must have felt flattered and overwhelmed by his urgency, so she gave in and married him.'

'Gave in? He was a honey pot she could not resist dipping her greedy little fingers into, for goodness' sake. Her father was a poor country squire with five daughters to marry off and nothing but their looks and eagerness to manage it with.'

'No wonder she had little choice about the matter, then, despite your father being thrice her age and frightening her with his passion for a seventeen-year-old girl.'

'Passion?' He repeated the word as if he thought it might be poisoned. 'He was the coldest fish I have ever met. Indeed, I have seen ones dead on a slab with more life in them than he had.'

'He does not sound very cold if he had her most treasured possessions burnt.' She pointed out a flaw in his argument, but he did not want to be reasoned with.

'Cold fury,' he argued shortly. He recalled feeling the full weight of that whenever he displeased the man, until Cousin Christian intervened and made sure Harry spent his vacations down at Garrard House.

'He beat her,' Viola defended his indefensible mama hotly, as if the woman was still a living, breathing person who mattered. Not to him, not when she had left him to live on here with the very man who beat her, if that fiction Viola had swallowed whole was true, of course, and he very much doubted it.

'He beat me and I was in no position to run away.'

'I am so sorry, Harry,' she said as if she meant it, and he did not want her to. Not today or any other day, for that matter. He did not want her to waste warmth and understanding on such a cold and dead cause.

'He is dead and I am alive and in full possession of all the things he hated the thought of me inheriting from him one day. I won, Miss Yelverton.'

'Have you, Sir Harry?' she said. Drat the woman, didn't she know this was the wrong time to be brave and bold Viola instead of the cool and efficient governess she ought to be whenever she was with a rogue like him? 'Did you really win, or are you still living your life by defying everything your father wanted you to be?'

'No, I am my own man. I do what I want, when and how I want to do it. He had no control over me from the day my Cousin Christian knocked him down for beating me unconscious when I was eleven.'

'He did that? What a brute Sir Alfred must have been.'

'Aye, and if I always do the opposite to what he did, then I should not go very far wrong.'

'You cannot let him dictate your actions even in that way; you will have let him win if you do.'

'I am sorry not to match up to your expectations, then, Miss Yelverton, but I refuse to live by anyone else's rules ever again,' he mocked her earnestness and felt shame curdle his belly even as he willed her to go away and leave him alone to lick wounds she did not even know she had inflicted on him. 'Now let's forget my folly and take a look at your own in walking into the lion's den this late at night instead.'

'You are not a lion,' she told him, as if he had disappointed her.

'No, I fear I am not,' he said with a sigh, and

the anger seemed to seep out of him as he met her eyes and saw puzzlement and worry in the summer-blue depths of them as she stared back at him with no idea how loudly her femininity called out to his inner beast.

'Your mother wrote to him, begging to be allowed just a glimpse of you in the distance,' she said and dragged him back into the unhappy past again, a place he did not want to go.

'I do not care, Miss Yelverton,' he said flatly and forced himself to disappoint her.

'Surely it must make *some* difference to how you feel about her?' Viola said, but even as she spoke, she wondered if his barriers were too high for anyone to be able to reach the true Harry she so badly wanted to know.

'Must it? I am sorry, but even if it is true, this is far too late for anything she wrote or said to make a difference to me.'

'But don't you see? All those years your mother was so desperate to see you she was ready to plead with a man who terrified her. She loved you very much, Harry,' she said, impulsively laying her hand on his, as if human contact might be enough to reach him in the chilly place he looked as if he had gone to at the very mention of his mother and the empty half of his miserable childhood.

'Obviously she must have done. From the way she took me with her when she fled the marital home, she clearly adored me,' he said bitterly.

'She knew he would take you from her and make you suffer for it if she even tried to take his son and heir away from him. But your father was not exactly the passionless man you describe him as, was he? Perhaps you misread her as well.'

He grimaced and the hand under hers tightened into a fist she soothed with a gentle touch to remind him he was no longer alone with the fear and possessiveness and frustration that had made his parents' marriage a private hell. 'Better if he was,' Harry said bleakly.

'We cannot alter the past,' she told him, then could have kicked herself for being so trite as he looked even more remote and alone with his memories and his parents' darkest secrets.

'Yet it can alter me? You expect too much if you think I will ever forgive either of them for what they did.'

'I know you will meet my expectations because you always do. It is your own you cannot deal with, Harry.'

He looked revolted by the very idea he could be author of his own isolation, and she suddenly realised that was exactly what it was. He was so alone and so aloof from the rest of the world behind his light-hearted manner and once careless ways. How could she ever have been taken in by his *what a fine fellow I am* confidence and that lazily rakish smile? He had been so alone until the children were dropped into his life to be cared for and engaged with whether he liked it or not. Her heart ached as she saw the boy who grew into this special and unique man at last. He was so lonely it made her life after Marianne left home look like a happy circus wrapped up in a picnic and topped off with an all-night party full of loved and welcome guests.

'I am not who you think I am, Viola,' he warned her with a note of danger and desperation in his voice that ought to make her step away from him, run back down the hill and leap into her lonely bed, but she had seen the Harry behind the barriers now. He should not be left alone inside them if there was even a chance he could find a new way of living without at least some of them dragging him down.

'And you are not who you think you are either,' she told him and tightened her grip on his tense hand to say she was not going to be brushed aside or fobbed off that easily. 'You are a good man, Harry. You are a fine guardian to your cousin's children and the most considerate employer a governess could long for in her wildest dreams,' she told him with a wobbly smile. There was so much else she dare not say and how she wished she could be his comfort and joy to offset the bleak and unhappy tale of Sir Alfred and Lady Marbeck's marriage, but that was clearly impossible.

'To hell with that,' he said, as if her attempts to bridge the past with the present revolted him. 'You have no idea of who I really am,' he added, as if he was furious about her ignorance.

'Then tell me,' she challenged and met his eyes with a glare of her own. She was tired of being good and quiet and doing as he wanted her to do and staying away. He was not an island; he was no harsh adventurer intent on taking whatever pleasure he could get wherever he could get it, then moving on without a second thought for any suffering he might have caused. He was not the man he pretended to be even to himself.

'Best if I show you. Then you might believe I am a savage at heart and leave me alone,' he said, as if she had driven him to actions she was not going to like one bit.

'I...' She was about to argue, but it was too late, he was too close and her words dried up on her lips. Then he was kissing her far too deeply and desperately for her to even think, let alone say anything.

So this was what Marianne felt, she heard her own inner girl gasp as if she was sixteen again and discovering all the best secrets of the universe for herself. No wonder her sister had left everything she knew behind to find her Daniel and stay true to what they had together if this was it. Impossible to turn your back on something as wonderful as this if there was even a chance of a future behind it.

Grown up and very adult as she was now, Viola still felt her breath stall and her head spin like a dizzy schoolgirl's. The vital life force in him spoke to the one in her and agreed on need and desire, and the very air felt as if they had to share it now—as if they could not breathe fully without one another any longer. Her knees wobbled and her head went somewhere new, but he was the strength and security under all the strangeness of this heady, achy feeling. He raised his head to gaze down at her as if he was trying to hang on to some reason she was delighted to see the back of.

'I can't pretend not to want you any longer,' he told her rather grumpily, as if he had to, as if this had been a long time coming for him as well.

'Of course you do,' she said recklessly and seemed a lot more ready to jump into the unknown with him than he was with her, bless the gallant great idiot. 'Ever since I arrived here and you lifted Emma down, then tried to hand me out of the carriage as if you thought I might not be able to manage it by myself, I wanted you to kiss me so badly it hurt,' she confessed.

'It's been as long as that for you as well?' he said as if it sounded incredible, but for goodness' sake, he was about as desirable as a man could get, so why wouldn't she lust after him in secret from the moment she arrived at Garrard House and realised what she had done in saying that first yes to him like a besotted idiot?

'That's how long since I admitted it to myself, anyway,' she confessed quite shamelessly.

'I burned for you from the first moment I laid eyes on you.'

'You hide it very well, then.'

'And I thought you were even more beautiful because you were trying so hard to hide it,' he said with a look that reminded her strongly of Bram caught in wrongdoing and trying to pretend it was someone else's fault, except obviously it was not.

'You did?' she said incredulously.

'I did. I told myself I was only begging you to come back here for Emma's sake, but I lied,' he said.

'So what was so special about me?' she asked because she was human after all and she badly wanted to know.

'I just saw you; Viola Yelverton, a woman with the girl still alive in her heart. I knew the boy in me was long dead and it was as wrong to want you then as it is now, but I want you like a desert wants rain, Viola. So you had best leave right now before it makes me dangerous.'

'I quite see how it might, after all this time, but I am still not going,' she said with a reckless come-hither look his reluctant confession had charmed out of her somehow. Despite looking about as reluctant to want a woman as any man could, he was admitting to it none the less. Mutual wanting sang like a siren song inside her and would not be quieted or damped down or shrugged away this time. 'I ached for you as well, Harry; I have counted off every day, almost hour by hour, until my two stupid years will be over and done with. It has been like carving lines into rock to keep on doing it day after day, as if I could imagine nothing better than not seeing you any more.'

'What a pair of idiots we are, then,' he admitted with the smile in his eyes she could never resist, and it did not matter if he was still guarding himself against her in his heart of hearts. They were as physically close as almost lovers could be, and his Aunt Tam and the children were a mile away and should have been fast asleep for hours by now.

'What about the servants?' she said, managing to snatch at a last gasp of common sense when he picked her up as if her legs could not be working properly after that devastating kiss, and as they were not, she felt quite unable to argue with him. She let her head spin in dreamy delight and anticipation of even more wonders to come.

'I sent them to bed so I could sit here and brood about you and the five months and nine days left until you are not the children's governess any longer and I ought to let you go.'

'Nearly one day less by now,' she argued with a glance at the shocked face of the clock in the hall when the master of the house walked past it with a mere governess in his arms. She had to smother an urge to giggle at it even though she could not be tipsy as she had not drunk wine with her dinner tonight. *I am drunk on desire and daydreams*, she decided as the feel of being held so close and carried so easily in his arms was pure wonder to her after all those days and nights of vicious frustration.

Chapter Sixteen

So, how did you make a man you had given everything you had to last night believe it was all a mistake in the morning?

What a question, Viola decided as she swam up through fathoms deep of sleep and sensual Viola the Lover collided head-on with Miss Yelverton the Governess coming the other way. She smothered a tender smile in the pillows of his grand bed as she shifted his heavy arm from around her waist and he grumbled something, rolled over and went back to sleep.

She shot the elegantly simple and expressionless clock on the mantelpiece of his grand bedchamber an enquiring look. How on earth was she going to get out of here without one of the maids or a sleepy footman knowing exactly what she and Harry did last night? He obviously slept far too deeply after making love to a very willing woman to worry about the details of her escape, and she didn't want him to anyway.

It was wonderful and strange to be his lover instead of an almost old maid, and she wanted to treasure the joy of it for a little bit longer, but reality was waiting for her on the other side of his bedchamber door and there was no point putting it off much longer. It would burst in on them if she stayed here, and he would have no choice but to offer for her to rescue her good name as best he could.

Well, he *would* have a choice, she decided with a lingering look at the back of his complicated head, and she only just managed to stop herself caressing his wildly disordered curls because it would probably wake him up and she preferred him to be asleep right now. Any other rake would have the choice of denying any responsibility and blaming her, but he was an exceptional one—in every way. His gentlemanly honour would demand he marry her and she had no mind to be pushed on him as an unwanted wife. There had been quite enough of that idea in her past, thank you very much, and he definitely did not want to marry her or anyone else.

She picked up her far-strewn garments, checked she had every single stitch and hairpin she came in here with last night and made sure there was not even a trace of her in his bedchamber for his valet to find. Then she tiptoed into his dressing room, very relieved that it was too early for that valet of his to be waiting there for his master to face a new day.

She used cold water from the jug left there last night to wash with. Squirming at the idea the man might know his master had spent last night with a woman, even if he thought Harry must have smuggled his mistress in there and not the governess, she used her chemise to dry herself on and did her best to think herself back into being correct Miss Yelverton again.

She took a critical look in the mirror and made sure she was neat and almost as composed as that lady ought to be at this time of day. If she could just get outside before anyone saw her, she could pretend she had been for a very early morning stroll after waking early and deciding she might as well. She was so far from her proper place she must remember to be surprised she had walked so far if anyone saw her near the house or in the park.

Her heart beating like a war drum, she very carefully let herself out through a neatly hidden door from Harry's dressing room and out on to the servants' staircase. She crept downwards like a thief in the night, or in her case very early in the morning. Getting outside unseen was the vital part of her plan and proved more of a challenge than the rest. She had to dart into a dark corridor and hide behind a vast cupboard to avoid a pair of giggling maids going down the backstairs at the start of their working day. Heart thumping even faster now, she stole back to the workaday parts of the house and, thank goodness, the kitchen door was closed and the back door unlocked, ready for any early deliveries.

Now all she need do was get back to Garrard House before Miss Marbeck and the children were up and nobody need know she might have been out all night. She would be as outwardly respectable this morning as she had been for every one of her life until today, even though today was different—today she was Harry Marbeck's lover. She hugged the secret magic of last night to herself and marvelled there was not even an iota of guilt in her as she finally crept out into Harry's deer park and let herself remember every lovely detail of being utterly desirable and completely wanted for the most glorious night of her life.

Harry had not slept so well for months. He lay on his belly with his face in a pillow and stretched contentedly. He had not felt this good for much longer than months, if ever. Of course he had never spent the night with a governess before, although he smiled sleepily and recalled they had not done very much sleeping. Best make up for it now, then, he mused hazily and nearly gave in to the delicious lethargy tugging him back into contented oblivion and daydreams of Viola's perfect skin and delightful breasts and tiny waist and just the right length of leg to go with her petite build and wrap about a man in the heat of passion.

Now he had to smother a groan into those pillows of his as the very thought of her keening out her desires and surprises and the lovely humour of them as lovers made him hard as rock. Except his brain was prodding him about all the urgent things he ought to get up and get on with. He would have to marry her, of course. Even a rogue like him could not bed

Miss Viola Yelverton, former governess and vicar's daughter, without offering for her the moment he had his clothes on.

Suddenly lying here with a satisfied smile on his face felt stupid rather than wonderful as he remembered that he did not want to be married, to Viola or anyone else. He sat bolt upright in his bed and this time he was glad she was gone, although he had known that the instant he began to wade his way up from sated sleep. Now he remembered the day he decided he was never going to get married in stark detail.

He had been at school and those rumours about his mother and her lordly lover stung so sharply he had written to ask Cousin Christian if they were true or not. He had trusted Chris to tell him the truth and he did so, regretfully and with an aside that Harry must try to understand his mama had always been too young and lively for an April and December marriage. In time, his father's possessiveness and jealousy had driven them even further apart than they were at the start of it. With his cousin's letter in his hands to confirm the awful truth—that his mother had whored herself to escape the old man—Harry had promised himself he would never fall into the trap they caught themselves in because he was never going to get married in the first place.

How did he feel about that promise now and the trap he was about to snare himself into because he and Miss Yelverton had not managed to keep their hands off one another last night? He sighed even in this sunny bedchamber with the fugitive scent of her teasing his senses and knew he could not blame her for leading him to where they stood now.

Despite her past as a very unhappy fortune hunter, he could not make her into a designing hussy when there wasn't a designing bone in her body last night as she confronted him with his mother's confounded outpourings and finally let her passionate nature off the leash. The lightness and generosity of their loving would not let him change her into someone else, but the dark mean little corner of his soul that hated the very idea of marrying her because they had lost control of their passions last night still wanted to.

Well, he had no choice now and he was sure they could make a good enough fist of the business if they both tried hard enough. If they put every effort they had in them into the project, they might not end up hating each other, he supposed, with a stir of hope in his heart as he reminded himself what an exceptional lady Viola was under all that starch and self-doubt. He recalled Reverend Yelverton's sermon at his son's wedding and told himself it was possible not to live in married strife. He and Viola had already proved they could raise children with as much love and understanding as they could hang on to while those children were doing their best to push them to the edge of reason in order to be sure they really were loved.

He was not his father and she was not his mother, thank heavens. They could do this, as long as they stuck to the rules and based it on cool reason and passion and left affection and tolerance to grow between them if they stuck at it long enough and refused to believe in fantasies and fairy tales.

Right, that was the future settled, then. Viola was sure to be worrying about her good name by now. She must have begun to worry about that the instant she woke up in his bed and of course she had gone before anyone was stirring to catch her tiptoeing out of his bedchamber with the dawn. He grinned at an image of her ghosting along the twists and turns of the maze of corridors added to the oldest parts of the house and hoped she was not still lost somewhere and working hard to come up with a plausible explanation as to why she was here at this time of day.

Then he imagined her still in here with him, luxuriating by his side and happy to indulge in some lusty early morning lovemaking. Such luxuries would have to wait until after they were married now. Viola would never want to be caught in his bed beforehand, so he would just have to resign himself to having no wondrous beginnings to his day until he got her up the aisle and put his ring on her wedding finger and with a special licence that could easily be done by the end of the week.

Whatever he felt about Sir Harry the married man and the Lady Marbeck he had sworn never to acquire, they had acquired each other last night and it was high time he stopped remembering Viola crying out his name in the extremes of passion last night and got up. Reverend Yelverton looked as though he would be having a very busy year, with all three of his children very likely to be wed before it was out.

* * *

'No, thank you,' the woman said so calmly they might have been discussing groceries or more books for the children instead of his only ever offer of marriage.

'The devil you will not!' Harry almost shouted and only got Miss Yelverton's best frown for his trouble and a sad shake of her head just in case the children were within earshot. They were not; he had made sure of it by sending them on a strictly supervised walk with half his household in attendance to make sure they stayed out there and did not get into trouble.

'No, I will not marry you, Sir Harry, but thank you for asking me to,' she replied so coolly he shivered and began to believe she really meant it.

'Why not?' he managed to ask past this bewildering sense that control of his own future had slipped through his fingers somehow.

'How can you even ask me that?'

'It is quite easy. I just plumbed the depths of my vast inexperience at offering marriage to a lady and found it a common-sense sort of question. We made love last night; we shared a long night of passion I could not even imagine enjoying with a lady of such upright character and virtue until I met you. And you were a virgin, Viola, so please don't try to pretend otherwise when we both know it will be a lie.

'I am quite ready to admit that I am a bad example of a baronet and not at all the sort of husband you or your family would like you to marry, but we can build a good marriage together if we try hard enough. It is all quite logical when you think about it, and you have always been an admirer of logic, have you not? Well then, logic says we made love and now we must marry each other, and you may have noticed that I want you urgently and, if the evidence of last night is anything to go by, you want me almost as lustily back.'

As he said it, he knew it was the wrong thing to say if he really meant to persuade her to be his Lady Marbeck. He wanted to curse his own clumsiness and ram his fist into a wall in frustration because this was not going at all as he'd intended. That sort of unleashed violence would make her even less likely to say yes to him and it reminded him too bitterly of his father for him to actually do it, even if she kept on looking at him with cool scepticism and her best governess mask of patience in the face of extreme provocation. These could have been the most important minutes of his life and he was making a mull of the whole ridiculous business. By trying to joke about her steely refusal to marry him, he suspected he had sealed his fate.

Now she thought he had only asked her to marry him because they got carried away by a passion so strong it was nigh impossible to fight any longer. And she was right, wasn't she? It was true that he wanted to do it all again as soon as he could persuade her to say this yes to him first. And he did not want her sneaking off into the dawn as if he was a guilty secret next time they made love. So it made sense for them to be married. It was all perfectly logical and she was the one who was being irrational and just plain wrong.

'No, there is nothing logical about it,' she argued all the same.

She had no idea how fascinating and desirable she looked even now as she avoided his eyes and tried to pretend she had no idea what he meant about that urgent, nigh overwhelming need and all the heady passion they had shared last night. She had no experience to guide her, he supposed and wondered if he was a poor lover despite the purring satisfaction of all the beauties he had cozened into his bed before this one.

'We are very different in outlook and station,' she told him earnestly. 'It would be a very unequal alliance, and I have no wish to be married to you because we lost control of our passions last night and you feel guilty about it.'

'It was not only the once,' he corrected her with a hot look to remind her they had been very carried away indeed last night. 'And I do not feel guilty about it. I am flattered you allowed me to be your first and last lover and am on fire to do it all again as soon as you promise to marry me afterwards. So why not tell me how you *can* be persuaded to marry me and I will find a way to convince you I am right and you are wrong,' he said, as if it was his dearest wish to marry her, but it wasn't, was it?

No, yet how could she have forgotten how eagerly they loved last night and not just the once. They woke in the darkest hour of the night and did it all again with such sleepy sensuality he ached for her just thinking about it. Perhaps that was why he had been so clumsy and she said no to his proposal.

'I cannot tell you how to achieve the impossible,' she said coolly, staring into the middle distance as if he did not interest her in any way now she had satisfied her curiosity about him as a lover. Perhaps he did not, he decided, cold creeping into him like a killing frost and an uncomfortable thump to the heart.

'I have all my teeth and do my best not to smell,' he half joked because he had no other way of coping with a sudden emptiness inside him he needed to ask himself a lot of questions about when he was alone with it.

'What high standards you think I have, Sir Harry. Yes, you do have them and, no, you are the cleanest gentleman I have ever encountered, and I am still not going to marry you. We lost control of our baser selves last night, but there is no need for you to pay for it with your freedom.'

Funnily enough, this did not feel like freedom. It felt bleak and unkind, and she did not look as if she was miserable as well. He might have to be angry about her wrong-headed refusal to listen to reason if that would not remind him too much of his chilly old tyrant of a father. 'What do you expect of your perfect husband, then?'

'Love,' she said starkly, then shook her head as if she knew it was unreasonable of her. 'Shared interests and common purpose as well, I suppose, but for the most part, I want what my sister had with Daniel and my brother has with his Fliss. I want that unlikely husband you speak of to share his warmth and passion and joy with me for however many years we have on this earth together. I want the impossible, you see, and I will not marry unless I can have something you do not believe in. So, no, I will not marry you, Sir Harry, but thank you for making me an honourable proposal, and you are now excused from taking a wife when everyone knows you do not want one.'

'But you have to. We made love,' he said numbly. 'We spent the night together and you gave me your maidenhead, Miss Yelverton, if you insist on having the truth with no frills on. I refuse to dishonour a lady and walk away with a smirk.'

'Forget last night; you have done the gentlemanly thing and offered to marry me and I have said no, so that is the matter over and done with and no harm done on either side. You can go back to your real life now and I can return to mine.'

'You cannot dismiss me as if I am one of my wards who did something wrong. I am a grown man.'

'I know,' she said, and for a moment there was a dreamy, remembering look in her eyes, as if she recalled exactly how grown up they had been together last night. Then she shook her head as if to say she was not anywhere near as impressed by him in the cold light of day. Stern Miss Yelverton was doing her best to pretend yearning, vital, sensuous Viola did not exist, and he still believed in her even if she did not.

'What will it take for me to change your mind?'

he asked impatiently as her refusal to see sense bit into his pride and something lonely he did not even want to think about.

'I have already told you,' she said with a sort of weary patience, 'and you do not love me, so you cannot.'

'I have ached for you from the moment I first laid eyes on you, you stubborn woman.'

'There you are, you see? I infuriate you,' she said, as if that proved he had only ever wanted her for her silky-skinned and finely curved body when he knew it was far more than that. 'You got what you wanted last night, Harry, and so did I,' she told him as calmly as if they had swapped books or played a game of cards instead of making love until he could hardly remember his own name for wanting her.

Even thinking about it had him in a pother, and he had to forget his manners and turn his back on her to resist a temptation to prove to her there was far more between them than an itch they had scratched by kissing her again and feeling her take fire in his arms.

'Do you really think this is me getting what I want?' he barked as he paced the room like a tiger in a cage. He was trying to deal with about the same level of fury and frustration as one of those, he decided, as that urge to put his fist through a wall came back and made him feel far more primitive and angry than he ever wanted to be with any woman, let alone this one.

'Do you think so little of me you imagine I do not still want you with every atom of my mind and body and who knows what else I might have to be tortured by for the lack of you? I saw the dreamy-eyed girl under the teacher that first day you pretended to be so stiff and correct in the spring sunlight with me. I saw all the things you do not want me to see and you called out to something in me I did not want to know about. Fair's fair, Miss Yelverton. You opened something hidden deep inside me, so stop looking at me as if I robbed you of some precious commodity because I cannot say a word I still do not believe in, whatever else we could mean to one another. You have made me a dishonourable man by refusing to wed me when we both know you ought to. What if you meet this mythical man you want to make all those promises to and you cannot because you gave your maidenhead to me instead of him? Between us we robbed your perfect knight of your perfect love last night.'

'Last night was not a crime,' she told him tightly, and he felt any advantage he had gained slip away as she silently accused him of making the most enchanting and memorable night of his life seem less.

Her inner Viola must have admitted it was important, then. He grabbed at that thought as she watched him as if she expected him to crawl out of the room on his slugly belly. Very well, he would go, for now, but he would try again when she had reflected on what he had to offer. She would be his desired, respected and interesting lady and, if he courted her doggedly enough, he was sure to win her over to the idea of being his in the end.

Chapter Seventeen

A month or more had gone by since her refusal of Sir Harry's proposal when Viola received the letter she had been expecting since Darius and Fliss's wedding. Marianne and her Viscount were going to be married on Christmas Day at Owlet Manor and her little sister simply had to be there to support her this time. Viola dashed off a delighted acceptance before it even occurred to her that she ought to have asked Harry for his permission to attend, but she had been doing her best to avoid him lately and Miss Marbeck seemed to assume it was a given she must go, so she did as well.

Her best figured muslin and the favourite satin-and-gauze gown she had worn for Darius's wedding were both going to be far too thin to wear for a Christmas marriage. So, knowing how much it meant to her sister for her to be there, Viola allowed herself to be nagged and reasoned into a trip to Cheltenham to find exactly the right material for a new gown for such a special day, and perhaps, just this once, it could be frivolously impractical.

A good thing she had already decided to indulge herself since she fell for a length of fine silk velvet in a delicious shade of cream dusted with a hint of rose pink to give it life and colour whenever light lingered in its softly draped folds. Miss Marbeck told her it would make up beautifully and if you could not be impractical at your only sister's wedding, then whatever was the world coming to?

Next they happened on a pelisse already made up for a defaulting customer and it could so easily have been made for her instead. Wasn't it wonderful to buy something that flattered her and made her feel young and feminine instead of a nigh-invisible governess? Viola dismissed an inner voice that sneakily asked who she wanted to feel young and feminine for and decided she loved the deeper and slightly more practical shade of the rose-pink wool, trimmed with bands of a deeper rose that was almost red in certain lights. All they needed now was a bonnet of sufficient splendour to crown her new outfit and perhaps Miss Marbeck and Emma might be satisfied she was going to be turned out to perfection at long last.

Except nothing would quite do for them and Viola felt slightly ashamed of herself for being the one who felt weary and a little bit jaded now they had spent a whole morning shopping. She was with a lady closer to seventy than sixty and a twelve-year-old child, for goodness' sake, and she was the one who was longing for a nice lie-down in a quiet room. The lady certainly seemed to be enjoying spending such a large chunk of Viola's savings on fripperies and showed no sign of the weariness that was dragging Viola's delight in her new clothes back down to earth again.

'I still like this one best,' Viola said after she had tried on more hats than she ever wanted to again and preferred the first one she had noticed in the milliner's window.

'Hmm, I am not sure. What do you think, Emma?'

'The shade of the ribbons and plumes is all wrong, but the shape does suit Miss Yelverton's face, Great-Aunt Tam.'

'Emma is quite right. It does frame you well,' Miss Marbeck told Viola, as if she needed permission to order one almost like it, but with different coloured trimmings. 'Do you guarantee me you will have one made up with all those fuss and furbelows dyed the exact colour of Miss Yelverton's gown?' she demanded of the hovering milliner.

'If we have a snippet from the modiste to match them to, then of course we can,' the woman said, and Viola was very happy to believe her. So she ordered her new bonnet and hoped they could now go home.

'Half-boots next,' Miss Marbeck said with a militant look at Viola to say she should not even bother arguing, because they were not going home until the entire ensemble had been perfected.

'I already have a pair of cream-coloured kid slippers that will do perfectly well,' Viola said to try to stop them spending the next hour or more at the bootmaker when she wanted to go home right now.

'Totally unsuitable for a December wedding,' her new fashion mentor declared grandly, so Viola meekly tried on shoes and half-boots dyed in delicious shades she had hardly known existed until today.

'Gloves,' Emma reminded her great-aunt when Viola unwarily gave a sigh of relief on leaving the bootmaker an order for fine suede half-boots in the same shade as the trim on her new pelisse. It was a ridiculous indulgence for just one day, but it was Marianne's wedding and she knew she owed it to her sister to make a special effort. The feel of that fine velvet moving as she did would make her feel like the woman Harry woke to her full potential on that autumn night that seemed far too long ago now it was almost winter as well.

Sometimes it seemed almost like a dream and she could hardly blame him for it not being repeated. He had asked her to marry him at every private moment he could make ever since and she still could not endure the idea of spending a lifetime with a man who had never wanted to love her and probably never would. Except she missed him so badly she had trouble sleeping and often woke up feeling weary and unwilling to face another day without him, but she would get used to it; she had to since she refused to marry the man and feel like the wife he had never really wanted to have for the rest of their lives.

'And you need a tippet to fend off the cold, and do not even try to tell me it will not be nigh freezing in that chapel Harry told me has lain unused for half a century,' Miss Marbeck informed her sternly.

'Darius promised my mother to have braziers lit in there every day of the week leading up to the wedding so my father will not suffer in the cold,' Viola said defensively, but felt that tippet loom anyway. She might as well be hung for a sheep as a lamb now she had got started and it was easier to agree with her two tyrant guides to fashion than spend even more effort arguing with them about it. After all, she did need new gloves and it would be nice to have a little extra warmth to add to the pelisse and it was a shame to spoil its elegance with the ancient woollen scarf she usually wore.

'Have you worn Miss Yelverton to a thread yet, Em?' Sir Harry asked his eldest ward with a wry smile as he lifted her down from the carriage several hours later. Viola knew he was nearly right when she longed for him to do the same for her, then take her into his arms and simply hold her until some of his energy wore off on her.

'Of course not. We had a wonderful time,' Emma said with a blissful sigh, as if outfitting her governess in prime style had been a wonderful experience for her and she felt invigorated by it.

Viola was glad for her pupil even as her feet screamed an argument. 'Emma and your aunt are certainly a force to be reckoned with when they work together,' she managed to joke as she waited for him to hand Miss Marbeck down, then got down on to solid ground herself without his help the moment his back was turned.

'I shall avoid milliners and haberdashers and mercers and mantua makers whenever I go near a town in their company from now on, then,' he said with a sharp glance for her behind his aunt's back to say he had noted her sly manoeuvre and did not approve. Even while he joked with the others, it still felt as if he was waging a private skirmish with her and it was so tempting to give in to fatigue and this odd sense of loneliness in company and succumb to being the other half of Sir Harry and Lady Marbeck. The ultimate loneliness of being married for the sake of his gentlemanly honour stiffened her spine as she made herself march ahead of him into Garrard House as if she had energy and to spare.

'Can you imagine Uncle Harry in your new bonnet and pelisse, Miss Yelverton?' Emma whispered with a delighted chuckle, and Viola had to smile at that very unlikely image.

'Not his colour at all,' she murmured and was glad to sit down on the nearest sofa at long last and be brought tea and scones as if she was the lady of the house home from a weary day shopping and not the children's governess. She had turned down the honour of being Sir Harry Marbeck's lady too often to have a right to feel wistful about not being so tonight, she reminded herself as the tea began to revive her.

She told herself it was better to be a governess for the rest of her life than watch Harry wistfully follow more attractive women with his eyes for the whole of their marriage. He knew far too much about feminine finery anyway. He would never stay content with her for long, and she refused to entrap him when she was the one who had truly let herself forget who they both were that night and simply surrendered to the terrible need that stirred inside her even more potently now she knew exactly what she was missing. She was a fool, she decided despairingly and made herself sit here and look as if he meant no more to her than the doctor or the baker or every other man who was not Sir Harry Marbeck and might as well be invisible, as far as she was concerned.

'Oh, isn't this *wonderful*?' Fliss asked as she smiled up at Viola and held out a hand to help her down from Harry's luxurious travelling carriage before the grooms could jump down and do it for her.

Considering her sister-in-law was even shorter than she was, Viola thought it seemed a very long way to the ground and blamed their joint lack of inches for the fact her feet did not feel very steady when she got them on to solid ground again at long last.

'Wonderful,' she affirmed with a squeeze of Fliss's slender hand, as if to thank her for the welcome and say that next time they met perhaps they would know one another well enough for a sisterly hug.

Right now she was longing for a few minutes' peace and quiet in the sunny room Marianne had worked so hard to make lovely for her when she came here half a year ago with Darius. Now Marianne was getting married again, and who could have dreamed any of this would happen when she came back from Spain a broken woman? Maybe there was a special magic in this mellow old house, years of frustrated need for a family and the love it needed to make it feel like a home again, perhaps? It certainly had a good feeling about it; this ancient manor Darius had never expected to inherit from their reclusive Great Uncle Hubert was hosting the second wedding this year after a drought of them for at least half a century.

'I must admit I did suspect something special was growing between them when I saw them together at your own wedding,' she told her fairly new sister-in-law as soon as the ground began to steady under her feet. Maybe it was like taking a sea voyage—after long enough in a carriage you became so used to the motion that having steady ground under your feet left you feeling off balance for a shaky moment.

'I was too taken up with it being *my* wedding to take much notice of how anyone else felt at the time, but you only have to see them together now to realise how deeply in love they are. They can hardly take their eyes off one another. I never thought my sober and dutiful former employer would ever manage to unbend enough to let the world see how much he adores his wife-to-be, but how wrong I was.'

'Love will do that to a man,' Darius's deep voice informed them solemnly, but with a hotly posses-sive look for his wife of three months on his face to prove it.

'You were far too good at creeping up on us when we were children,' Viola accused her brother and walked straight into his offered bear hug, feeling as if their last one was only weeks ago instead of far too many years gone by. She had been aloof from her family far too long and returned his hug warmly, then laughed as he lifted her off her feet and spun her around before setting her on her feet again.

'I have missed you, Darius,' she murmured and felt tears warm her eyes, but blinked them away with a mock frown. 'You always would insist on carrying me about like a rag doll when I was little.'

'You are a bit too big for me to do it now, although you always will be my little sister to me and you must admit you are still the littlest of us three.'

'I am a lot bigger than I was,' she told him with a mock grimace at Fliss over their shared lack of inches. 'Does he do it to you as well?' she asked sympathetically.

'He is only allowed to sweep me off my feet when I say so,' Fliss said with a fierce look for her husband to say that was not now.

'And I always take her orders as a challenge,' Darius said cockily, and Viola could see exactly why their marriage worked so well.

They were compatible in so many ways she felt that nasty little stir of jealousy raise its ugly head again and stamped on it hard. She and Harry might be physically perfect for one another—she knew they were so even more strongly now she had truly learned how to ache for him since they made love far too long ago—but they were not in love. She knew how perfectly their needs could mesh into a beautiful, fiery lovemaking, and wanting to do it again was a constant hunger in her body and mind that was sapping her strength and making her afraid she might give in and do what he wanted her to just to get herself back in his bed again.

Yet it was their minds that would not let them be a declared and committed pair of lovers. Harry was too guarded, too damaged to tease her and challenge her like Fliss and Darius did one another, or offer her love and comfort and to do his very good best to sate this heady, seemingly insatiable need that haunted her even more now she was fifty miles away from him.

So where was she with today? Ah, yes, love was written all over these two and look how happy they made each other. Perhaps that was what hurt the most—knowing she could not make Harry happy. She was not enough to make him forget his appalling childhood or show him what a fine man he had made of the neglected and abused boy he once was. Only he could take down the blockade against love he had put up when his mother left and his father treated him as if he blamed his own son for his wife's failure to love him back.

What a stupid, self-obsessed and carelessly cruel man old Sir Alfred Marbeck must have been. He had distorted Harry's inner picture of himself out of any resemblance to the real man Viola knew and loved. There, that was it. She had admitted it to herself at last. She loved him! She must have paled and felt herself waver in her tracks again as the very ground seemed to shimmer and shake under her feet. The full truth and folly of how she felt about Sir Harry Marbeck hit her so hard no wonder it felt as if the world was about to shift on its axis.

'Catch her, Darius!' She heard Fliss's sharp order, and the panic in it snapped her back to here and now.

'No, it's all right. I am perfectly well,' she told her brother as he looked as if he was about to pick her up after all. 'Truly I am. I suppose the journey was longer than it was in the summer when the roads were dry, and my feet do feel horribly cold after spending so long in even a very comfortable carriage. In fact, I think they might refuse to hold me up altogether if we stand out here much longer getting them even colder.'

'Come inside, then, so Fliss and Marianne can fuss over you and sit you in front of the fire until you are nigh roasted. If we can find my other sister and get anything past the haze of love and dreams she is wrapped up in nowadays, that is. I had better go and try to make her realise you are here again, at last.'

'Is she living here again until she is married, then?'

'I suppose you could call it that,' Darius said ruefully, with a glance up to the second-floor window where Marianne had chosen a lofty bedroom when they came here, as he offered Viola his arm to help her up the broad front steps to his fine old house. Fliss took her other side just in case Viola toppled, and it felt so good to be part of a family again.

Viola's heart lifted as she realised she would always have the love and support of her brother and sister and their respective partners for life. She might not have the man she loved and yearned for in her life for very much longer, but she would always know there were people who loved her in a very different way and it made her a lucky woman. Rather luckier than she felt she deserved as she thought of Harry with his prickly Aunt Tamara and the children to love him, but nobody there to support and adore him as only a true lover could.

Chapter Eighteen

Harry was restless. He had Aunt Tam and the children under his roof, and the whole place had been swept, cleaned and polished until he wondered if he was even allowed in it himself. Now it was decorated with every bit of evergreen the children could cram in, and spices and oranges and pine cones scented the air. There were feasts planned, revels to be looked forward to and Cook could hardly move in her own kitchen for the vast amounts of food to be stored or got ready or given away. This would be a Christmastide like no other he could remember at Chantry Old Hall, and the children could hardly contain their excitement. Yet still he felt restless, and it was so late on Christmas Eve now that Aunt Tam was in bed, the children were finally asleep and he had a chance to pace the grand old rooms of his grand old house made festive and glowing for the season and miss Viola in every one of them.

He had to keep himself occupied somehow, so he

ordered his butler to send everyone to bed and settled in the library, telling himself he might as well be restless there as anywhere and he did not feel like facing his bedchamber without Viola in it just yet. Why had he chosen the library? he wondered dourly as thoughts of their most memorable meetings haunted him almost as strongly in here as in his lonely master bedroom. Because he liked to torture himself with the memory of kissing her in here before Bram had his accident, perhaps?

Then there was the night she came here full of hope and compassion and with his mother's secret journals in her hands, believing they would change his mind about so many things when all they would do was prove his mama was as silly, self-obsessed and flighty as he had known she must be ever since he was old enough to realise why she left and did not take him with her. Still, Viola thought they were important, so he ought to read them some time, even if it was only to tell her that he had the next time he begged her to make an honest man of him, to show her he had listened to her pleas to do so.

Where had he put the confounded things, then? Somewhere nobody else would find them, he recalled thinking as he put them away as irrelevant the day after his passionate midnight encounter with Viola and her first refusal to marry him. He was so distracted at the time he had a job to remember where that was now. Filed under D for distracted or V for Viola? No, I for impossible, he recalled all of a sudden.

'Cynical, perhaps, but there you are, my sweet Viola,' he muttered to himself like a lunatic. 'A cynic is what my darling mama made of me, and not even you can put her right again, as far as I am concerned.'

How he wished she was here to argue with in person about his dearly departed mother, dearly departed to the protection of her noble lover and never mind the self-serving outpourings in these slender little books he was still trying to persuade himself to read. He had to do it, and Viola was at Owlet Manor to watch her sister marry Alaric, Viscount Stratford, so if he wanted to argue with her he would have a long way to go. And three very disappointed children in the morning when neither of them was here to wish them Happy Christmas.

'Right, then. Stay here you must, so you might as well get on and read the damn things, Harry,' he ordered himself.

It took a while to get the measure of his mother's handwriting. She had crammed a lot of it into three slender books, so it cost half a beeswax candle and some eye strain, but by the time he read to the end of them, his heart was aching nearly as much as his eyes. Had he fooled himself his mother was much older than she was when she married Sir Alfred, then? He did his best not to call the old man his father even before he read the tale of a seventeen-year-old girl ordered to marry a man more than thirty years her senior by her own father. So that was a harsh and unfeeling grandfather on the maternal side to add to the list of ancestors he did not want to resemble in any way.

An image of Viola at seventeen, pushed out into a social world she was too young to properly under-stand, slipped into his head and made him even more revolted by that cynical bargain those two old men struck over his mother's head. Thank heavens Viola had had the stubbornness and strength to fight for her freedom when her mother tried to push her into a similar marriage with any man who could afford to keep Viola and her parents in comfort. He had met the woman at Darius Yelverton's wedding and even then he thought her a puzzle.

Mrs Yelverton had probably started out with those good intentions the road to hell was paved with. He imagined she loved her family and wanted the best for them, but for her the best was a rich husband for her youngest child and a settled home when the Rev-erend Yelverton had to retire early for the sake of his health. Best for a middle-aged couple with money worries and two absent and endangered older chil-dren must have become the best for Viola as well in the woman's head, and that was the part of it he could not understand. With her head full of dreams and hopes that went against everything she was being told to want at seventeen, the world must have felt such a terrifying place for Viola, and yet she had the bravery and hope to break through it and make a life for herself as a teacher.

He sat and stared into the dying fire and brooded about parents and children and all the damage they managed to do to one another. He scowled at the silk-bound writing books with their girlishly tiny writing and tapped one of them against his knee as he tried to work out what reading the first two changed. His mother was barely eighteen when he was born, and the first book was full of a girl's hopes for her unborn baby and the loneliness and fear of her strange new life.

Sir Alfred looked both familiar and strange to Harry through his mother's eyes. She wrote that her husband was more passionate and possessive than she wanted him to be, but it was after Harry was born and Sir Alfred's nearly insane jealousy of her absolute love for their baby manifested that she really began to change. At first Corinna Marbeck was an almost doll-like wife whom her much older husband could mould. Then Harry was born and she grew up.

It felt odd to realise he was the rival for his mother's affections whom his father had come to hate, but her growing fears for Harry as he went from baby to toddler to boy seemed so vivid they touched even his guarded heart. He could see why Viola had been moved to tears by this tale of a desperate young mother more or less alone against the whims and obsessions of a still powerful and sometimes dangerous man.

Any mild liking his mother had for her new life as the wife of a rich and important man soon evaporated. She had poured out her revulsion and hatred for her husband in these slender journals and done so in such tiny writing that Harry suddenly knew the old man would not have been able to read it with his failing eyesight. He would also have been far too proud to let anyone else read it aloud and hear her true feelings about the marriage that must have been more like a prison sentence to the girl whom he expected to simply do as she was bid when he married her.

Clever of her, he decided and smiled wryly at the notion his mother could have been so much more than Sir Alfred would ever allow his young wife to be. Of course that was not the sort of marriage his father wanted and the law made it impossible for his wife to leave her husband and take Harry with her. Legally she was Sir Alfred's chattel as surely as if she was a dog or a horse.

When she wrote about having to lock Harry in his nursery with the nanny at night and hide the key so his father could not get at him, Harry began to see why a mother might do what she did to try to push Sir Alfred's hatred on to a true and adult rival for her affections instead of a helpless child. She seemed to think if she was not here Sir Alfred could not be able to blame Harry any more for all that had gone wrong in their marriage.

'Too much to hope for, Corinna,' he corrected her twenty years on, as he still could not bring himself to call her Mama. The old man hated his son to his dying day, but holding on to Harry was his best revenge on a runaway wife who had run to a more powerful man so he could not take his feelings out on her.

Harry was so caught up in the tale now that, although he heard the clock strike two, he could not make himself put the last of his mother's journals down and go to bed. Instead, he read the last book with its tale of his first five years of trouble and turmoil, noting she picked up her pencil less as her troubles grew darker. Words could not put a barrier between her and her husband or protect her son, so perhaps the comfort of them grew less as her life seemed more and more comfortless. And all this went on while he played and ran wild about the stables and farms rather than inside where his father raged at him if he even dared speak.

Since there had never been any sympathy between him and the old man, it was not so hard to turn it on his mother after all. Who would have thought a few bits of thin paper would bring on such a turnaround, but he was ashamed to realise his revulsion against his mother was always on his own behalf.

Six years of living with a monster, of taking the blows meant for her son and pretending to the rest of the world all was serene and lovely at Chantry Old Hall? He felt sick even at the thought of her so young and alone with such a raw dilemma to work her way through. No wonder her lord appealed to her as an alternative and she had so desperately hoped that with her gone the wedge between father and son would go, too. After all, the old man must have married her to beget an heir and now he had one.

Sighing bitterly for the almost insane reason why his father had hated him until the day he died, Harry decided Sir Alfred was right about one thing: he was too much like his mother. That felt good as he laid the last book down and reached for her letters. Who would have thought he would ever be able to say that and really mean it?

And who could have put them in the secret drawer of his mother's writing box in the first place? Not his father; he would have put them on the fire. Now he came to think about it, there was a scorched edge to one, as if it had been rescued from burning. Hmm, he must have words with Aunt Tam about all this one day and find out what she knew and why she had never told him. For now, though, he might as well finish up his mother's words and finally go up to his lonely bed and try to get some sleep before three excited children woke him up with the first glimmer of midwinter daylight.

It was a beautiful wedding, Marianne and Alaric's Christmas Day celebration of their love and commitment. All the more so because Reverend Yelverton had all the time in the world to marry his eldest daughter to her besotted Viscount Stratford. As the little chapel on the estate had only one Christmas marriage service to host and this was it, he had no need to scurry through it and on to the next couple and the next, then the next.

Most vicars and curates would be busily marrying all their parishioners who had been unable to wed during Advent today. Then there were the couples who only had this one day a year to marry, then have a whole day off to celebrate. Viola felt the unfairness of their hired labour acutely for a moment

before the joy and love of Marianne's second wedding day blotted out any other thoughts but joy for
the very happy couple.

She was supposed to call Viscount Stratford
Alaric now, but something about him made her knees
want to curtsy and her tongue call him nothing less
respectful than Lord Stratford. Marianne would be
just a little bit less happy if she did, so somehow
Viola would bend her tongue around Alaric's given
name and teach herself to see him as her sister's
much-loved husband until he hardly seemed like a
viscount at all.

But she missed Harry so much today that it hurt.
The last time one of her siblings was married in this
miniature church, with its age and simplicity to make
it feel solemn and kindly somehow, Harry was at her
side to put a bubble of joy inside her that made every
moment of the day special. Today there was only the
ache of his absence, a wistful longing for him that
was not simply physical, although heaven knew that
was bad enough. She felt not quite complete and less
than happy now he was not here to make her feel
she was always on the edge of a splendid adventure.

Harry was only a breath or so away from Viscount
Stratford in title and riches, but somehow he was a
world away in ease and humour and in the way his
bright blue eyes made her want to laugh with him.
Then there was his natural charm, and that was even
before she added in the way his tawny hair misbe-
haved when he was not paying it close enough attention and the mischief in his eyes when he focused on

her as if she was the only person in the world who truly understood him.

There was his wry smile when he was silently agreeing with her that the world was inclined to folly and wasn't it a good joke they both understood the full humour of it? Quite a long list when she came to think about it, she decided, as she closed her eyes and tried to remember how it felt to have him stand next to her and make her feel gentle and hopeful and ready to dare almost anything in his company.

'Viola?' Fliss whispered.

'Sister dear, do pay attention to the matter in hand,' her brother murmured in her ear, and Viola realised the wedding was over and she had not been paying proper attention to the heartfelt vows of her sister and her beloved Alaric. Now the bride and groom were triumphantly walking out of the little church together as man and wife and Darius signalled to her that she should walk ahead of him and Fliss in Marianne and Alaric's wake. As the guests clustered outside in the frosty air to watch the bride being handed up into the wedding carriage for the very short journey to the house, they even managed to look warm enough to linger outside and kiss as they stood in a beam of late December sun.

'Please ignore him. He is quite impossible,' Fliss told Viola with a roll of her dark eyes for her impossibly beloved husband when he poked his little sister in the back to get her to move out of the way so he and Fliss could enjoy that brief beam of sunlight as well.

'I know,' Viola agreed and only half-heard the

cheers when Marianne tossed her wedding bouquet not at all randomly, but straight at her. Viola had to hold out her hand to catch it or be hit smack in the face by the tight little bundle of forced flowers and evergreens.

'You next,' Fliss said lightly, and suddenly that was the right answer to all her questions and confusion these last few weeks. Her life felt right for the first time since she and Harry made love and she decided to complicate it with scruples and confusion and turned his repeated offers of marriage down.

At least Viola felt certain of who she was and what she wanted as she returned the jokes and nudges of her family and Darius's neighbours with a laugh and a smile that felt wide and real and warm for the first time today. She did not care what they thought of her marriage prospects, or lack of them, and she did not need to worry about her brother and sister any more. Marianne and Darius were both blissfully happy, so she could stop feeling guilty about them, and Marianne clearly did not care where she lived, as long as she was with her beloved Alaric.

Darius and Fliss had found their true home here, mainly because they were living in it together and wherever the other was that was home. This was Darius's unexpected inheritance and he richly deserved it, but they would be content in a cottage. Viola felt the love and pride of generations was almost alive inside the wide roof timbers and generous banks of diamond-paned windows, but Owlet Manor was not her home.

For her, home was not a single place she would yearn for if she was ripped away from it; it was a deep emotional bond with a person that made it so for her. And that person was Harry. He was her home, whether he liked it or not, and somehow she doubted if he would, despite all those demands she marry him. Making him her centre and her life might be too much of a commitment for him to feel quite comfortable with, but somehow they would find a way, because that was what they needed to do for one another.

Knowing how her world truly span at long last made the rest of the day pass in a daze for her. She must have laughed and eaten and toasted the bride and groom and she could vaguely recall making excuses not to dance because the idea of spinning about the room on a variety of strangers' arms made her feel sick and dizzy. At last she was so weary she could not keep up the pretence of heady gaiety any longer and wished Fliss a quiet goodnight before she slipped away to her peaceful old bedchamber and waited out the darkness until she could think of a way to get back to Harry in the morning.

Darius had let it slip they thought Fliss could be carrying a child. Of course Viola was delighted at the thought of a niece or nephew, and her mother and father were overjoyed at the idea of grandchildren at long last, even as Fliss did her best not to overshadow Marianne and Alaric's special day. Viola grimaced at the discomfort Fliss said she had been experiencing and her mind flicked through the list Viola's mother had reeled off to confirm whether her daughter-in-law was indeed with child.

Viola sat up a little bit straighter on the bed and felt shock slam into her as she mentally recited that list again now. She had been dreamily brushing her hair and trying not to miss Harry so much she knew she would not sleep tonight. Bouts of dragging tiredness, spurts of equally inexplicable energy, nausea first thing in the morning and sometimes later and, if she smelt certain smells or turned too suddenly, this odd sensation of losing her balance, then feeling it come back again no sooner than she had almost lost it?

'Oh. My. Life!' she exclaimed to the peaceful air. Marianne had made this room ready for her as a sanctuary for Viola, should she ever need it. 'And goodness knows I do tonight,' she whispered.

She recognised every one of those symptoms because she had been suffering from them herself after she and Harry made love so gloriously and recklessly. No, surely it was too soon to tell if she was carrying his child? Two months and two weeks, she added up hastily and shook her head. Not too soon after all, then, she guessed. She could not consult her mother about the chance she was growing Harry's child in her belly in her turn, though, could she? She shuddered at the very thought of her mother's hysterics if she had as much as a suspicion that her younger daughter might be with child and not in the least bit married to her baby's father.

She ought to be shuddering and having hysterics herself right now, but somehow she could not drum up the energy. Instead she pressed a wondering hand to her flat belly and felt warmth and wonder bloom within her as she longed for it to be true. She wanted Harry's child with a passion she would not have believed she could feel for such a tiny maybe baby, one who might still be a product of a slight cold and a wistful need to feel his child grow inside her.

Well, if it was real, she would love it as he had so needed to be loved as a child himself. Her baby would know its mother loved it from the moment it was born until she took her last breath on this earth. With a tender smile, she imagined Harry's reaction to its very existence and knew he would love it as much as she did. Never mind his father's selfish reaction to his own son, her Harry was his own man and he would make a wonderful father.

Once upon a time she might have been fearful at the thought of being with child outside marriage and ashamed of herself for giving in to overriding passion, when she ought to know the consequences as the daughter of a country clergyman, but then she met Harry and he changed her in the blink of an eye, even if it did take far too long for her to accept the difference between Miss Yelverton, the wary governess, and Viola, the joyous lover.

She knew Harry would stand up for them; he

would even do his best to love them. He had done
it for his cousin's children and he would certainly
want to be there for his own child. How he would
feel about that child's mother she had no idea, but
he would marry her anyway. That was enough for
her, then; she loved him and she could not imagine
him ever telling any other woman that he loved her,
so that was all right. She would have his honour and
respect.

Now she somehow had to get some sleep as well.
She owed the baby she might be carrying more than
she expected for herself. So she finished brushing
her hair, bound it up into plaits, slid between warmed
sheets and blessed Fliss's housekeeping and consideration for a sister-in-law she hardly knew. Lying
in a feather bed in her brother's lovely old house
as the timbers settled and creaked around her—as
if they were having a desultory conversation about
an eventful day—Viola forced herself to breathe in
and out slowly and calm the excitement of her racing
thoughts. In less than seven months' time she could
be a mother, they insisted eagerly, and she grinned
like a fool into the friendly darkness. Her, a mother?

Well, who would have thought it when Sir Harry
Marbeck came to Miss Thibett's exclusive academy
for young ladies in search of a proper governess for
his orphaned wards? Certainly not her—Miss Yelverton did not dare look beyond the narrow confines
she had chosen for herself back then, but she did now.
She looked and then smiled yet again into a profound
winter darkness that was not going to tell anyone

her secrets. She knew her future held Harry, and she loved him so much that having a little less than her brother and sister had found this year hardly seemed to matter in the grand scheme of things.

Chapter Nineteen

'I need to go home, Fliss,' Viola told her sister-in-law the next morning when they met at the top of the stairs, both looking and no doubt feeling a little pale and delicate at this time of day after the trials of early morning. Viola met Fliss's dark eyes without bothering to raise her own defences and did not care if Fliss knew the state she was in or not. Somehow she knew Fliss would not judge her, but supposed she must now find a way to stop Harry being confronted by a furious Darius demanding to know why he had failed to marry her after getting her pregnant.

Viola finally agreed with Harry that their marriage must happen whether he wanted it to or not, and he might not even want to marry her any more after all her contrary refusals. 'I must get back to Chantry Old Hall as soon as I can,' she said. 'To Sir Harry and his family,' she added, as if that explained everything, and perhaps it did.

'Where else would you want to be at Christmastide?' Fliss said, as if she had already been expecting to have to find a way to help Viola get back to the Cotswolds this morning.

'I knew you would understand.'

'I do, but I was not quite sure you did yet.'

'I love him, Fliss. I think I must have done after seeing him with his wards and realising how much he loves them. I have no idea why I thought I was excused from falling in love with a handsome rake when I accepted his offer of employment, but longing for him all those months without realising exactly why has certainly paid me back for being so arrogant.'

'That sounds a very long time to pine for a man as dashing and easy to love as your Sir Harry sounds when you talk about him,' Fliss said with a smile that really did understand how a woman could fall for a contrary and stubborn great idiot and still manage to fool herself she had not.

'It was, and I only failed to stamp on my own hands to keep them off him the once.'

'Did you? What a strong woman you must be, Sister-in-Law,' Fliss said with a wicked smile that admitted to Viola she had not kept hers off her own dashing hero very often after they realised they loved one another.

So that would be from a month or so before their wedding and right up until today, from the look of her delighted smile, then. Oh, dear, when it came to the adding up easily scandalised gossips would do after the birth of both their babies, Viola had no doubt which of them would prove most scandalous. She spared a brief qualm for her mother, who would find out soon enough what her younger daughter had been doing this autumn with the most handsome and desirable man she had ever met. Their first child was going to be born several months before he or she ought to be if only the poor little mite had proper and respectable parents more able to resist extreme temptation when it came their way.

'Not noticeably,' Viola admitted with a joyous smile and a smug hand laid on her still very flat belly that mirrored the gesture Fliss was making with hers. 'Where Sir Harry Marbeck is concerned, I am weak as water.'

'When you are in love with a man, I see little point in being any stronger than you need to be. You two obviously have so much wasted time to make up for it is no wonder you cannot wait to go home. Making up for lost time is vital between lovers, don't you think?'

'I do and it is still wasting,' Viola said shamelessly.

Luckily Marianne was so absorbed in her bride-groom, and he with her, they had hardly left their bedchamber since they came back from their own wedding to notice anything odd about Viola's suddenly longing to depart the next day. She smiled at their frank delight in loving one another in every sense of the word now they had got around to it.

If only she could do the same, a wistful voice piped up to almost spoil her much quieter hum of happiness at the idea of being Harry's wife and the mother of his child. No, she was not going to have doubts like those ever again. Darius and Marianne both had loving and passionate marriages now, but she and Harry could build on what they had until it was more. And one day Harry would realise a family could be happy together and know he would never turn into his father if he lived out his century.

With Fliss's goodwill and energy behind her, as well as her own eagerness to be gone as soon as possible, Viola was soon installed in the grand travelling chaise the Viscount and Viscountess Stratford would not be needing for some time. That disgraceful pair had barely found time to open their bedchamber door long enough to say the odd sheepish hello to their family and eat the food left outside it for them.

At least Viola did persuade them to answer her knock on the door, so they could agree to her blithe suggestion she and their coachman could give their team a good run by taking her to Chantry Old Hall as fast as they could get there. The carriage would be back again before they could even miss it, she told them, and of course they were far too absorbed in loving one another to care a hoot where it had gone.

'Go on, then, if you feel you must,' Marianne urged from behind her new husband, who was pretending not to be naked but for the door between him and the outside world. 'It is high time you realised how much you love the man.'

'Does everyone know that but me?'

'No, I don't think he does either,' her sister said with a challenging look as if to say *And why is he among the last to know, Viola?*

'Then I had best hurry back and tell him I will marry him after all,' she said out loud.

'Yes, I do believe you had. Perhaps you should convince him you love him before you tell him about anything else you may have forgotten to mention,' Marianne said with a challenge in her eyes that told Viola she was not so absorbed in her new husband she could not put two and two together and make four.

'We do have a great deal to talk about,' Viola said serenely and hoped Darius was feeling as puzzled about that part of her life as Alaric looked when he found enough attention to meet her eyes instead of concentrating on the feel of his naked new wife plastered against his back like a cloak.

Daylight was in very short supply at this time of year, so Viola was on the edge of her seat, silently urging the careful coachman on by the time darkness began to fall by mid-afternoon. Willing the man to go on as they had got as far as Marbeck Magna, she dreaded him deciding the climb was too much for the team they'd hired in Worcester to make without a night's rest at the village inn below Chantry Old Hall. That would feel bitter indeed when Harry still felt as far away from her as if they were two or three counties apart and she dared not risk taking a tumble in the dark if she tried to walk up in her condition.

She held her breath as the carriage slowed on the way through the village and only let it out again as it gathered speed for the climb and the coachman coaxed and cursed the horses into bracing against the weight of the beautifully made and not all that heavily laden vehicle. She gave a sigh of pure bliss as the honey-coloured stone of Chantry Old Hall came into view, basking in the last rays of winter sunlight lingering on high up here and out of the shadow of the hills.

She truly would not care if Harry lived in a hovel, as long as he was willing to let her share it with him and his wards, but it was going to be a constant delight to come back to this lovely old place whenever Harry realised how much his house and estates and all the people who worked for him needed him to be here. She had resigned herself to leaving it, knowing how he had once loved city life and his dashing society friends. Now the children were settled and feeling secure again, he was sure to want to be with them again. They would have to spend a good deal of time in London and Brighton and at all the grand houses his circle of friends frequented when they were not in town for both of the social Seasons.

When she was not too busy bearing and tending their children, she hoped he would want her to go with him, but when she was with child, he would probably want to go on his own. She already felt a yawning gap threatening inside her at the thought of him miles away from her, in every sense of the word, enjoying himself with his grand friends and a fine mistress and all those flirts the gossips said he could charm by the dozen. Still, she would be the one he came home to. She was the woman who would bear his heirs and was already working on the project for

him if he did but know it. Her unique place in his
life already felt precious, and he did not even know
he was going to be marrying her yet.

'Oh, hello, Miss Yelverton. You're back at last.
We're playing hunt the slipper,' Bram said breathlessly as he only managed to avoid cannoning into
her by some neat and rather anxious footwork on her
part and him skidding to a halt that nearly sent him
into the nearest branch of evergreens instead.

'Are you indeed?' Viola said a little breathlessly.
Fear had leapt into her mouth fit to choke her as she
wondered how much damage a racing boy could do
to the tiny baby she now felt certain was growing in
her belly. In that moment she knew how much she
wanted Harry's child. Even if he amazed them both
by deciding he did not want to give up his freedom
for her or his child's sake after all, she would still
want it. If he did decide not to tie himself to a vicar's
daughter who would always expect too much of him,
she would find a way to keep their child.

She had powerful connections by marriage now
and Alaric had more houses than he knew what to do
with. He was sure to be able to find her a secluded
one where she could stay to bear her child in secret,
then claim it publicly as a dead relative's child without a home and bring it up on her own. He and Marianne were already planning to shelter waifs without a
home, so she would be an older version of their waifs,
with an extra one of her own on board as a bonus.

'Who won?' she asked as soon as she had got her

breath back and worked that important part of her life out in her head. If Harry was not as pleased to see her as she was to see him, she would have to make a plan to steal away from here before the child began to show. Waiting out the full three months left in her contract would not do, she decided as she added up five and a half months and knew she would not be able to hide her child by then.

'Sir Harry,' she greeted her lover breathily as he ran into the wide hallway and came to a jarring halt not quite as dangerously close to her as Bram's had been. She sounded like a besotted schoolgirl faced with the object of her sighs and desperate affections and decided she ought to be a little more grown up about it. 'How do you do?' she enquired with exaggerated politeness and felt even more foolish when he eyed her as if he had never seen the likes of her before.

'Very well, I thank you,' he said just as stiffly.

If Bram was not here, would he succumb to the same urge that was telling her to throw herself into his arms? Or was he embarrassed to think he had nearly had to marry her and now they were back to governess and paymaster again and thank goodness for that. Whatever he might be thinking behind that façade of his, she saw with dismay how many of his defences were back in place against her as he proved unreadable and was obviously nowhere near as pleased to see her as she was to see him.

'You are too late to help make the Twelfth Night Cake. We did that on Christmas Eve,' Bram said, as if all the excitement Viola felt when she was coming up the hill and along the endless-seeming drive had drained out of her and was now being added to his.

'Did you remember to put in the bean and all the other things a proper Twelfth Night Cake ought to have?' she asked because Bram deserved her attention and it did not look as if Sir Harry wanted it.

'Of course we did. I hope I get the bean—I want to be king for a day. Uncle Harry can be a knight, but you shall be my queen, Miss Yelverton, because Lucy would fidget all the time and Emma would try to make me do what she says, even if I was a king and supposed to be in charge of everybody.'

'Am I the best of a bad lot, then?' she teased him, and if only she could be as easy with the tall and silent man listening to them as if most of his mind was elsewhere.

'Did we ever find that slipper, Bram?' Harry suddenly asked, as if he had only just remembered what they were doing before she came to his home, instead of tactfully waiting for the children to return at Garrard House. 'Or either of your sisters, come to that?' he added, looking around as if it was an effort to think about what had been happening before she had arrived. It seemed a better sign than any he had given her so far, and a spark of hope rekindled in Viola's heart. It was Christmastide, after all, so who knew—they might yet manage to both be happy about the notion of being tied to one another for life at the same time.

'I bet Lucy sneaked into the kitchen,' Bram said,

and he was probably right. Lucy did like her food, and there was plenty of it in the groaning pantries and packed larders at this time of year. 'Lucy had better have stopped her fishing about in the Twelfth Night Cake for the king's bean or I will smack her for it since you never do, Uncle Harry.'

'Nor will you, young man,' Harry said with an effort that warmed Viola's rather cold-feeling heart. He looked as if it cost him almost as much effort to keep his mind on anything but her as it did her to stop thinking about him. 'Try it and you will find yourself upstairs on Twelfth Night with no chance to be king even for a day to worry about,' he added as Bram sped towards the kitchens with a militant look in his eyes.

'You will have to catch me first,' Bram said, as if not at all impressed by the threat of being stuck in the nurseries while the rest of them enjoyed the revelry and fun of a world turned upside down for the day.

And he was probably right, Viola decided. Harry would not have the heart to confine the boy on that day of all days, even if he did try to smack his little sister—if he succeeded in getting close enough, which Viola very much doubted he would, given Lucy's talent for being somewhere else when retribution for her sins was on the way.

'Later,' Harry told Viola with a regretful glance back to make her feel a lot deal better about her decision to tell him he was her lodestone for life and never mind how he felt about her, she would still marry him.

'Yes, later,' she agreed and followed him down the hall to the kitchen and, hopefully, the rest of the family. *Their family*, she thought dreamily, with a return to her buoyed-up mood of this morning and all the way here as fast as Alaric's horse could go. Emma, Bram, Lucy and whoever this little one she was carrying would turn out to be were going to make up a family Harry could love without limits.

'Glad you've come to fetch this little imp out of my kitchen at last, Sir Harry,' Cook said sternly, but peering past his broad shoulder, Viola could see a plate of rout cakes on the previously spotless kitchen table and Cook's pretend frown with affection underneath it. Obviously Lucy knew it was there, too, since she went on eating her treats.

'Miss Yelverton is back,' Bram announced importantly, and Harry moved aside so the others could see her.

'Oh, lovely; I'm so glad you will not miss the rest of the Christmas revels,' Emma said and dashed from her corner of the table to wrap her arms around Viola's waist in a hug Emma only gave to those she truly loved. Once again Viola had to tell herself not to be silly; babies were not the fragile little flowers she was suddenly imagining they might be and she truly loved this girl back, so she returned the hug and kissed her.

'It feels so lovely to be back,' Viola confessed with a happy sigh and a shrug for Harry's carefully watching gaze to say she truly meant it. 'I missed you all and at such a joyous time of year as well.'

'But you have your own family and we must not be selfish,' Lucy said in parrot fashion—clearly either Harry or Miss Marbeck must have been telling her so while Viola was away. 'Did the Viscountess wear a crown?'

'No, love, she wore a bonnet and a nice warm cloak with a blue velvet gown, and the Viscount did not wear his coronet either, before you ask. Remiss of them, I know, but that's the dictates of fashion for you,' Viola said and almost spoiled it by laughing when Harry rolled his eyes at her, then pretended to be solemn as a judge again for Lucy's sake.

'If I was marrying a lord, I would wear mine whether it was the fashion or not,' Lucy said disgustedly.

'A proper lord would never ask a restless little flibbertigibbet like you to marry him, and even if he did, you would never keep it on long enough to get married in it because you fidget too much,' her brother told her scornfully, and of course after that battle commenced.

By the time Emma and Harry had got between them and restored order, it was properly dark outside and the children were borne off to the Chantry Old Hall nursery Harry had ordered relocated to the main bedroom floor and decorated especially for them. They seemed used to the routines of the night here already and Viola had to tell herself it was only three days since she left for Owlet Manor and not the weeks it felt like now she was back again.

Even so, it was a long drawn-out business getting all three of them to bed, then persuaded to sleep with Carrie's help. The children were full of the revels to come on Twelfth Night and all the excitements leading up to it now the more solemn and reverent rituals of Christmas Day were over and they could enjoy the less spiritual parts of the Christmastide celebrations.

At last all three were asleep and Viola and the nursery maid exchanged relieved glances as they tip-toed out of the children's respective bedchambers. She was free for the rest of the evening, Viola realised with a skip in her belly to remind her she had a very important conversation to have with the master of the house. Carrie went off to a cosy-looking day nursery to sew and knit and do whatever she did every night now she was in charge of the nursery and no longer had to defer to Nanny's authority and gloomy prophecies of doom. Viola loved her pupils, but she was very glad she was not responsible for them all night as well as most of their days.

Carrie had grown into her role since that awful day in the summer and Viola knew she could rely on the girl to listen for a murmur or cry from her charges and not flit downstairs to flirt with a groom or under-gardener the moment the children were asleep. She wondered if Carrie would marry one of those besotted boys or decide to look after another woman's babies and not ruin her neat figure with incessant childbearing until she actually loved one of them.

Soon there might be another Marbeck baby to demand round-the-clock attention from its mother and a nurse, Viola thought as she paused on the stairs to grimace at the thought of what the servants would whisper about her when they found out she had a baby growing in her belly at this very moment and not the hint of a wedding ring on her finger.

Chapter Twenty

Harry heard Viola come downstairs at last and was even more thankful his Aunt Tam had gone to bed early. Viola looked weary and vulnerable tonight. Perhaps she had attended too many family weddings lately and been drained by all the excitement and emotion. So why did she hurry back here in Stratford's carriage when he was supposed to be sending his own travelling chaise for her the day after tomorrow? It had taken him such a huge effort not to tear off to Herefordshire after her, even with the children and Aunt Tam to be a proper nephew and guardian to over the Christmas season.

The bustle and joy of this time of year still had pockets of sadness in it for them; they all felt the gaps Christian and Jane left in their lives at this time of year when families gathered to remember and celebrate and say too much or pull caps and do whatever they usually did together. Chris and Jane had been his family when the one he was born into failed him, and this year he resolved to forget the unhappy past and remember them instead.

The children, Aunt Tam and Viola were his family now. They had built one around Emma and Bram and Lucy and he wanted them all at Chantry Old Hall at this special time of year, but he wanted Viola here most. He wanted her here always—at his side, in his bed and arguing with him, laughing with him, re-arranging all their lives as she thought they ought to be and simply being the true centre of his world. And every time he even suggested she might like to marry him, she looked at him as if he had said something distasteful and refused to discuss the idea any further.

So, yes, he had missed Viola as if a vital part of him was being torn up by the roots and dragged off to Owlet Manor with her. But he felt the limbo of the last weeks must end one way or the other almost as sharply. They could not go on with this charade of polite distance, not with all the passion and frustration and hurt underneath it bottled up like lava in a volcano. Something had to change soon, before the children sensed their tension and felt less secure and confident in the new life he had tried to build for them after their parents died.

For all the frustration and bitter bewilderment of the last two and a half months, he could not bring himself to wish he had never set eyes on Miss Viola Yelverton. As he watched her walk towards him in the lovely ensemble Aunt Tam had bullied her into buying for her sister's wedding, he felt his heart turn over because she looked weary and almost fragile under the richness and beauty of that gown.

This obviously was not the time to demand a reckoning when she looked as if it was costing her an effort to hang on to her usual serenity. Something must have happened while she was away and he did not quite believe the journey back to Owlet Manor without him was what rocked her world. That would be too much to hope for after all the weeks and months of trying every way he could to persuade her to marry him and being refused and avoided and just plain ignored. He had resolved to demand a once-and-for-all yes or no from her and he would offer her freedom from that devilish bargain they had made for two years of her life if she said no.

But now that she was here and he had his chance to face her with a *go as a governess or stay as my wife* ultimatum, she disarmed him with a new vulnerability and distracted his inner rake with a silky velvet gown that was not quite cream and not out-and-out pale rose either—a bit like her silken skin underneath it, he recalled lustily. The wretched stuff certainly emphasised every move of her delicious body as she moved towards him, looking not quite sure if it was safe for her to be Viola tonight, but here she was anyway.

He swallowed hard, reminded himself of the caution and weariness in her eyes when she arrived back here without any explanation as to why she was two days early. She must have a reason for making a hasty journey back. Did he dare hope she had missed him?

He watched her shadowed eyes and slightly wistful-looking mouth for clues and badly wanted to draw her close and kiss her. Then he could gently soothe her into telling him her thoughts and feelings and why she had rushed back here so impulsively. He might even manage to simply hold her and offer comfort, rather than ravishing her delightful mouth with hot, sweet kisses until she yielded everything they both wanted and was truly his Viola again.

'Have you dined yet?' she asked, as if she still wanted to keep him at arm's length with the trivial details of everyday life.

Frustration burned inside him at all the petty little social tricks adults used to keep their real emotions battened down. He was tired of her throwing them in front of him at every turn. 'I thought I might as well, since Cook told us you were eating supper with the children and Aunt Tam was hungry,' he said with a fragile sort of calm he was holding on to by the fingernails.

He really wanted to ask her if she had missed him half as much as he did her. Only as much as he would have a limb or so, or a vital organ, he reminded himself. But she looked as serene as an Italian Madonna now she was here and sitting elegantly upright on a chair as far away from him as she could get without actually leaving the room.

'Aunt Tam and Emma were right about that gown. The colour looks better on you than anything else I have ever seen you wear,' he said, secretly delighted she had donned it tonight instead of retreating behind her dull governess feathers as soon as she crossed his threshold.

'You never notice what I wear.'

'I could describe every item in your wardrobe down to the finest detail,' he argued, then frowned as he recalled some of them and wished he could not. 'For the most part, it is as fine a catalogue of what a poised and beautiful young woman like you ought not to wear as any I ever recall seeing.'

'Except this one?' she said with a provocative gleam in her glorious blue eyes he truly hoped he was not mistaken about.

'And the one you wore for your brother's wedding. I could almost be insulted you only bring out your fine gowns for family weddings and leave the rest of us to endure the sight of you in all that grey and mud and nothing-coloured stuff you insist on wearing the rest of the time.'

'I am the governess,' she told him, as if that explained everything, and he supposed it did, in a way. She was his governess, though—no, his wards' governess—and he supposed he was considered dangerous, so that explained the disguise. In fairness, he really was dangerous as far as she was concerned. He had bedded a lady under his protection in the most protective form of the word, then failed to marry her afterwards, even if it wasn't for lack of trying.

Maybe she was quite right to try to conceal her glorious figure and lovely hair and her piquantly beautiful features from his inner wolf when she came here, but he had seen past it to the true essence of her and wanted her anyway. She might as well have worn her finery from the start and spared them the deliberately plain stuff she thought would cool a man's ardour if he ever noticed the vibrant young woman under the governess's shell.

'You must marry me,' he said impulsively, and even as he kicked himself for saying what he had just promised himself not to, he had started, so his inner idiot decided he might as well carry on. 'I need you,' he added truthfully, because he did, in every sense there was.

'Need?' she said, eyebrows raised sceptically as if she was only accepting one meaning and it was nowhere near enough for her.

'Yes, need,' he snapped back impatiently because he was very close to the end of his rope and she ought to know it by now. 'I need you to wed me and bed me and make me feel whole again, Viola. I needed it the night we became lovers, as if we were two halves of a better whole, and I need it even more now. So, yes, I need you and I also need you to marry me. Lucy, Bram and Emma probably need you as well, but I need you as much as I need to breathe; I need you with every part of me there is to need with, Viola. I do not always have the words or the warmth or the steadiness you seem to expect of me, but I have always needed you and I always will.'

'And that is all you need, is it?'

'No, damn it. I need *you*, Viola. Just you and only you.'

'Hmm,' she murmured, as if weighing his urgent

reasons up in her clever mind and deciding it still was not enough.

'I want you, then, as well as needing you; I value you and am beginning to feel any life I might have without you is not going to be worth living.'

'Apparently you have always thought you do not *need* a wife. You seem to have been very sure you did not want or intend to marry one at all.'

'I had not met you then,' he explained impatiently. How could she not know she was the blessing he did not deserve? Suddenly the word fell on to his tongue as if it had only been waiting for him to realise who she really was in his life. 'Damn it all, Viola, I love you,' he said past a hoarse place in his throat that had always refused to use that word to anyone except the children until now. 'I love you, Viola,' he added more urgently and found out it was easier with practise. 'And please, will you just get on and marry me?'

'Promise me you are not saying so to persuade me?' she said, as if she really thought he might be.

'No. Why on earth would I say something I promised myself I was never going to say if I did not mean it? I do love you, Viola. I love *you*,' he said exultantly, and the surprise of it, the gift of it, warmed bits of him he had not known were so cold until they were warm and alive again. 'I am not my father or my mother, and loving you will not turn me into either of them. And I do not intend to run away and leave any child we might have one day alone and bewildered the way I was. Nor will I ever treat him or her as if everything that has gone wrong in my life since the day they were born must be their fault.'

It was almost too much to believe, Viola decided as a new and wonderful shock added itself to all the others she had had lately. 'Really, you mean it? You truly love *me*?' she asked, feeling dazzled and still unsure miracles happened to ordinary people like her.

'Why the emphasis? Why not you? It was you from the first moment I saw you, after all, and if only I was bright enough to realise it all those months ago, we could have saved ourselves so much heartache and trouble. If I had courted you from that moment on and you had seen what a handsome and charming fellow I really am, we could have been happy together for months and months. You, my darling, are one of the most beautiful women I ever set eyes on and you are kind and wise and true with it. Indeed, you would seem nigh on perfect to me if you were not quite so starchy.'

'I am *not* starchy,' she corrected him, then realised she was being exactly that by latching on to the one part of his speech that sounded like a criticism. She thought a lot harder about the rest of it and her heart began to race and her thoughts dashed about like idiots. 'And I am much more ordinary than you seem to think,' she warned him shakily.

What if he did not believe she loved him back when she told him why they should hurry up and marry one another to give the child she was carrying his name? He might remember his dark suspicions of women who only wanted mercenary things of a husband, as he thought his mother had from a rich man. With that idea in his head and blocking his good heart for so long, would he decide she only wanted to marry him to save her good name and give her baby one it need not be ashamed of? *Fool*, she raged at herself for not realising he was her love and her real life and all the things she truly wanted long ago.

'And I love you, Harry. I bullied my new brother-in-law into lending me his splendid carriage so I could race back here and tell you so, but now I am here, I do not know how I am going to persuade you to believe it.'

'Why not? It sounds a perfectly sound idea to me.'

'You might not think so when I tell you the other reason why I came home so hastily.'

'As long as you came back and you call it home, I am content,' he said impatiently and strode over to stand in front of her. She had to put out her hand to stop him before he swept her on to her feet this time and stopped her saying anything else with hasty kisses. It was so tempting just to let him; to stand up and wind herself around him like a vine and simply latch on to him and let everything else just happen in its due course. She could pretend her pregnancy was as much of a shock to her as it would be to him when he began to notice the extra fullness to her breasts and her bouts of dizziness and tiredness.

'I believe I may be with child,' she said baldly

instead, before she lost her nerve and that cowardly idea began to seem more and more attractive.

Silence, still and hard and somehow horribly empty, sank down on this comfortable old room as she watched him retreat into himself and brood. 'You do not want it,' she said flatly after too many seconds had limped by on leaden feet.

She should have known it was too good to be true. The singing happiness she had secretly longed to know ever since Marianne practically danced away from her sixteen-year-old self that night to seek out her Daniel and marry him sagged in mid-skip and fell flat on its face. She wanted to cry and rage and stamp her feet, but she was not sixteen any more. She was a mature woman who was about to be a mother and life was there to be faced with all its little triumphs and horrible, horrible disappointments.

'Of course I do,' he argued gruffly. 'Are you sure?'

'No. How can I be?' she was stung into demanding. 'Do you think I have some magical power that means I can see into my own womb and examine it for babies?'

'I don't know. I have never been a father before. You know your body a lot better than I do—thanks in part to your refusal to marry me for the two and a half months since we made love and, apparently, a baby.'

'I have never been a mother before either,' she said and heard the defensiveness in her voice and felt tears threaten. No time for them, she told herself furiously and dealt with what was, rather than what might have been. 'I thought the dressmaker in Cheltenham could not be as wonderful as she was made out to be when this gown arrived the day before I was due to leave and it felt much too tight in the bodice. I believed I was suddenly so very weary at times because of all the alarms and upsets before Darius's wedding and then…' She let her voice trail off as they both thought about the 'then' she meant.

'I found your mother's box and her letters begging to be allowed to see you and all her confused thoughts about you and Sir Alfred and you did not believe her, Harry. Then we made love and I wanted you so very badly I could not help myself urging you on when you would have stopped and recalled I was a prim virgin if I gave you the slightest chance to think about what we were doing to one another that night.' She paused and searched for the words that might make him understand why she had let down every guard she had with him that night, then raised them like defensive weapons in the morning and kept them there ever since.

'I must have been a very clumsy lover,' he said flatly, those stony barriers stark in his dear eyes as well now. She knew she had to abandon them completely and let him see the real, vulnerable Viola she had felt the need to hide even from him after that spectacular fall from grace.

'No, you were everything I ever wanted, more than I knew I wanted because I knew so little about wanting until you taught me how.'

'You soon learned to forget what I showed you, then.'

'No, I remember every second, every move we made, every touch of you on me, every inch of you inside me and all that heat and light and glory you showed me, Harry. I have replayed it night after night in my dreams, sleeping and waking. I cannot get you and being your lover out of my head.'

'Then why the stony no after no after no when I begged you to marry me? Why run away the moment you woke up in my bed and why keep on running until my child in your belly finally forced you to stop?'

'That wasn't what stopped me. I stood still and realised I had been running away from you when I ought to be running towards you before I realised the symptoms of early pregnancy Fliss has been having are much the same as the ones I am experiencing as well. I found out I loved you when I was stepping down from your carriage at Owlet Manor and nearly fainted on Darius's grand new carriage drive in front of him and Fliss at the shock of it, or at least that was what I thought at the time.

'It was only later I realised I might be carrying your child and he or she might have something to do with the fainting part of my moment of truth. So when I stopped and thought properly about why I was feeling so physically odd, as well as missing you as if a crucial part of me had been ripped away, I had to come home and tell you I think I am with child and I need you even more than I did before.'

'Love or need, Viola?' he said in a stark parody of her earlier question to him, and she regretted doubting him now it felt like steel slipping into her heart and coldness seemed to wash over her in waves.

Chapter Twenty-One

'Love every time, Harry,' Viola whispered and wrapped her arms around herself to try to warm her shivering body. 'Always love,' she added and made herself meet his eyes with all she felt for and about him unguarded in her gaze at last because this felt like her only chance to convince him.

'You would never lie about love,' he said, and her heart raced again because, oh, thank the heavens, it was not a question. 'Not about something so important to you Yelvertons.'

'Never, and if you like, I will tell you I love you every morning when we wake, even if I am about to be wretchedly sick in the mornings.'

'Yes, then, I accept that pledge and will hold you to it. I will need some convincing after all these weeks of longing for you in my bed every morning and every night and most of the time in between,' he said with all the hot intent of those weeks in his eyes along with a gruff knot of frustration because the father in him said no.

'We could be gentle with one another,' she suggested with a secretive sort of smile, and now she was shivering for a very different reason as she looked up at him with greedy, laughing eyes.

'If you knew how much that could cost me, you might not be so blithe and bold about it, Miss Yelverton,' he growled at her, and how she loved him for being so grumpy and rueful about the hot need in his brilliantly blue eyes and the slight shake in his hand when he pushed it through his hair and left it looking truly windswept, but probably not in the accepted fashion his stylish friends would recognise. She reached up an even more shaky hand than his to smooth it into some sort of order and instead made matters worse, revelling in the life and energy of his determined-to-curl tawny locks, as if everything about him was infused with his unique spirit and thus irresistible to her.

'Lady Marbeck,' she corrected him dreamily, and for the first time in her life, she felt the confidence of love given and returned as she challenged him to disown her under that name, since it was the one he always used for his mother when he could bring himself to call her anything at all.

'Not for three days,' he argued, as if he was perfectly easy with the idea after all.

'Three?' she asked in a voice squeaky with shock.

'Yes. It takes ages to get a special licence, don't you think?' he said blandly, and she almost had the giggles from all this see-sawing emotion as she saw him smile and it warmed all the bits of her that were not already warmed right through.

'Ages,' she confirmed throatily and smiled right back.

'And once I have one, I suppose we had best scramble back to your brother's house and hope your father and mother are still there. Do you think they have room for us two and Aunt Tam and the children as well as my coachman and grooms and anyone else who can find an excuse to tag along for our wedding?'

'There are attics and they might well have already begun work on the nursery and I am sure the children will be thrilled if they have to sleep in any odd nook and cranny Fliss and Darius can find them.'

'Aunt Tam will not and nor would I,' he murmured with all the ideas he had about making love to her with most of his tethers in place sensuous and suggestive in his eyes.

'Three whole days?' she asked and wriggled herself and her fine velvet gown against the delicious abrasion of his gentlemanly waistcoat, superfine evening coat and the delightful breeches he wore in the winter because this was an old house and it did have the most unexpected draughts and, ooh, here was one, she decided wickedly as she smoothed her exploring hands under that coat and round to the silken back of his waistcoat and the impressive bands of muscle and deliciously male Sir Harry underneath it.

'I never said we had to wait that long for one another, just for one another as man and wife. Not a lot of point in us pretending we can keep our hands off one another when the evidence we cannot will soon be on show for the world to see.'

'Not *all* the world, Harry,' she protested as he retaliated and ran his hands over parts of her where she was desperate for them to go. 'You make it sound as if I will be a prize cow to be eyed up and assessed for possible calving dates by all and sundry.'

'How shocking,' he murmured as he turned a few tables on her by shuffling her round so she had her back to him and he kissed the back of her neck, sending shudders of pure need down her spine, and this time her knees wobbled for a very different reason than they had been just lately as he murmured something appreciative and trailed kisses in places she had not known were so responsive and sensuous until now.

'Ears?' she said huskily as his tongue trailed havoc around the curlicues of one of hers and she moaned with need and delight.

'Hmm,' he husked in a manly rumble she could actually feel against her back where they were plastered together like, well…lovers, she supposed.

Since his provoking, teasing, glorious hands were busy shaping her breasts, slightly fuller than last time, and that 'hmm' had become a hum of sensual approval, she wriggled even closer to him and hoped nobody else was about to hear her sighs and little panting moans as he palmed her aching nipples so gently the suspense was nearly killing her by the time he settled to just enough pressure to make her

into a begging, sighing, wanting bundle of sensa-
tions. She felt as if she could swoon with heavy need,
as if every inch of her was aroused and wanted and
needed and here was just the man to sate it for them.

'Harry.' She managed to gasp a protest as his delicious touch left her nipples begging and aching for
more and he splayed his hands on her still concave
stomach. There was possession and pride and rev-
erence there, as well as even more fire in her deep-
est feminine core and such heat between her wobbly
legs she wondered how she would stop herself simply
bursting into flames before they got anywhere near a
bed, or a convenient *chaise*—any flat surface would
do. It did not even have to be flat, she corrected herself frantically. Just anywhere, she silently begged
him as the hot eagerness of his manhood behind her
felt as desperate and incapable of waiting any longer as the heat and excitement and breathless need
inside her was for him.

'Now,' she demanded on a hoarse, hot moan that
hardly sounded like her at all. 'Here, now,' she urged
as he still held on to those tethers of his long after
hers were broken and forgotten.

'Stop wriggling before I take you standing up,
woman,' he ordered her so brusquely she knew those
ropes he had clamped on his need and mighty desire
to just plunge into her and spend himself were close
to breaking point.

She thought about it for a moment and shrugged
because anywhere would do for her right now and if
he thought it was possible she was willing to try it.

'No, not for you,' he gritted out as if she had said that out loud and the effort of refusing her was costing him dearly. Somehow he got them to somewhere that felt soft and just the right height before he broke and hastily gave her exactly what she wanted. Yet even when he was inside her at long last and they were galloping together like racehorses at full stretch, he did everything he could to protect her from even her own urgent need.

He did not drive into her so much as dive with her into a smoother, gentler rhythm than the one she remembered from that first night they had loved and made the reason he was being so tempered and fluid with her it felt like all the care and love and promise she had ever needed all rolled into one exquisite lovemaking. His care for her and the baby said all the things they had been too awkward and tongue-tied to say to one another for far too long. It said he really did love her and would love their child and any others they had as well as the ones they already had. If it said anything else she was too busy to listen for and put aside that thought for later because he was so good at this she could not think at all any more, just feel.

Now she had caught the long, heady rhythm of him and moved with the subtle dance of love and frantic need and sex, for a moment they were poised on the edge of complete fulfilment and she felt triumphant and glorious. Every inch of him and every part of her was them and not her or him. They rocked one last step up to the top and flew off, free as air, sharp as falcon's wings, together in every gasp and moan and blissful glide back to the reality of being all and everything to one another she had never dared dream of before. He even found a way to gentle their joyous convulsions as they coasted down to some sort of earth again, even if it was not the same one they left.

She felt changed by this loving. The last time had changed her in very drastic ways they would still be wondering about years on from that first glorious October night. This time changed everything she was and would be. This was love and this was her and Harry bonded for ever, always united. Even if he did sometimes drive her demented, and she knew he would tease her to the edge of fury at times, she knew him too well to doubt it now. She would try to order him and the children about and they would poke fun at her managing ways and they would be a family together. That was what families did, or at least the best of them did, and they were going to be the best.

'I love you so much, Harry,' she mumbled in a hoarse, love-shocked murmur rasped by whatever words she had gasped out in the extremity of her passion and his.

'I know. You told me and whoever else was listening so time and time again just now,' he responded with a smile that went right down to his boots, or it would if he was wearing any. She was relieved to discover he had toed off his gentlemanly evening shoes before he took her on the sofa and she supposed their novel position had been for the benefit of their child, but it felt very much for hers as well as she snuggled back into his arms and turned her head to smile up at him as a very contented lover. Which was what she was, of course. Then his words drifted through the haze of contentment and sated desire and smug joy in what they had just done.

'I did not!' she argued, horrified at the idea half the staff in his household might have been listening while she panted and moaned out her feelings for this great idiot she could feel laughing at her back even now. 'Did I?' she added with a horrified look back at his face to hope at least some of the servants had gone to bed.

'A good thing I shut the door,' he answered with a self-satisfied nod at the ancient piece of elaborately carved wood that was always going to have a special place in her affections from now on.

'Yes,' she said as she wondered if even that closed door might have given them away for what they were and shrugged. She really did not care who knew she loved this man, was obsessed by a need to prove it to him as often as they could make a chance to, and with three children and a fierce aunt in the family even before they started on their own, those might be a lot trickier to find from now on, so she might as well make the best of every one. 'At least if it is a boy it will not be saddled with all the names of your close female relatives.'

'No, they would not suit him at all.'

'Idiot, you know what I mean.'

'I do, and if we have a daughter and call her after one of them, we will have to add all the others, and

I don't think the poor little mite will deserve all that, so we will have to think of a different one.'

'It could be a boy,' she said dreamily.

'Would you mind if I wanted to call him after my cousin?'

'Christian, you mean? No, I would not mind that at all,' she said with a tender smile for this bold lover of hers with his heart as soft as butter. 'I love you, Harry. I love you for the good man you are, whether you want to be one or not.'

'If it means being patient and saintly and waiting until tomorrow night before we can make love again, then I most certainly do not.'

'Oh, I think perhaps you can be good and I can be bad and sleep in your grand bed tonight and every night from now on, Sir Harry. What a wicked woman you are marrying—some people might even describe me as a designing hussy.'

'Not in my hearing,' he said shortly.

'I certainly have designs on you,' she said, turning about so she could kneel between his legs and kiss him fully on the mouth.

'I don't want to wear you out now I have got you at long last, love,' he said as soon as he could. She could see care for her and their child in his regretful expression and wry smile.

'Lucky I do not wear out that easily, then,' she told him.

All the candles had gone out and the whole of the rest of the house felt as if it was asleep when they finally tiptoed up the wide oak stairs, silencing giggles as he pulled and pushed her past boards that creaked and doors that moaned. At last Sir Harry Marbeck and his lady were safely in his grand master bed and Viola went to sleep in her lover's arms with a smile on her lips and all she had ever wanted to feel real and alive in her heart. She was going to wake up to see her love looking back at her and that was all that really mattered.

'My love,' she muttered as she finally drifted off to sleep in his arms.

'Ah, love, who would have dreamed a vicar's daughter could tame a rogue like me,' he murmured and joined her in dreamland because with the pace of his life as a family man he needed all the sleep he could get.

* * * * *